pause

Micki Fredricks

ROMANCE AUTHOR

MICKI FREDRICKS

Camie
Nice to meet
you at NIBB 2023

Micki Fredricks

Dedicated to my nephew, Lance Corporal Cody Jeffery Haley

1996-2017

I will speak your name. We will never forget. Until we meet again...

Semper Fi

ONE

TREY O'BRIEN HAD ALWAYS LOVED SPRING IN THE Midwest.

The cool breeze from his open truck window washed across his face, taking with it the memories of the harsh winter months. There was something about those first few days of the season. The ones when the sun felt surprisingly warm on his skin and made him buzz with excitement. He wanted to think it was the promise of new beginnings but knew it was more likely the promise of bikini season just around the corner.

He strummed his fingers on the top of his steering wheel, smiling as he rested his arm part way out of the window, and turned up his favorite country song. He'd been driving these dirt roads his entire life and was confident there wasn't a gravel road within a thirty-mile radius he didn't know by heart.

Looking around the cab of his old Ford truck, he ran a hand over the worn leather seats. So many memories had started right here. Wild nights with high school friends his

Mama still didn't know about. And adult nights with wild women his Mama would never want to know about.

He shook his head, laughing to himself remembering all the times he had driven these roads with people piled into the back of this truck. The goal was always the same; look for a place to pull over and drink whatever alcohol his best friend, Andy, had lifted from his grandpa's liquor cabinet.

He missed those days.

Life would be a lot easier if he could go back to a time where all he had to worry about was what girl he wanted to chase around this small town after his baseball game.

"Every man should be lucky enough to have a truck like this," Trey thought to himself.

He turned down the gravel road heading toward his family farm. He and his brother, Jamie, had been working this land since they were old enough to walk. Their father, Jed O'Brien, made sure his sons were on a tractor practically the moment they could pronounce the word.

Trey's heart swelled with pride as he slowed his truck to look at the newly thawed soil that had been in his family for four generations now. Even though he longed for simpler days when his responsibilities didn't weigh so heavily on him, he knew he was blessed to have been born into a family whose roots were buried deep in this community.

Trey was barely out of high school and Jamie just twenty when Jed's early death six years ago had thrust the boys into manhood. They had no choice but to take on the farming business their dad had spent his entire life building. Yes, they'd been groomed since their toddler years to take over the farm, but neither of them had been ready.

They'd fought and clawed their way through the last six years. They had bled together, butted heads, and made some foolish decisions, but they always stood united against the people who thought they would fail. At the end of the day, they were brothers, and there was nothing more important than family.

The farmhouse that had been his home for the first twenty-three years of his life came into view. Eve O'Brien stood outside surveying what would soon be her award-winning flower garden. She was not only an amazing woman, strong and resilient in the face of her husband's death, but also known to everyone as a master gardener. She was quoted in the Worth County Gazette as saying, "I never feel closer to God than when my hands are in His dirt."

It was a difficult decision for Trey when he moved out last year. Eve had assured him she would be okay and over the previous year she had flourished just like the rest of them. Hosting monthly parties for her book club, spending time volunteering, and offering the farm up for several charities to hold their yearly fundraisers. It seems she had found her passion. Hosting events and helping others is what made her happy and that's all that mattered to Trey.

But he couldn't get over the feelings of guilt he had every time he thought about leaving her alone in that big house. He often wondered after they all went home at the end of the day; did she walk the floors of the O'Brien homestead and feel lonely? Did she long for the days when he, his brother, and their friends filled the place with a level of rowdiness only teenage boys could bring? He knew she missed her husband terribly. He and his brother tried to fill the void in her life as much as they could, but they could never fill the empty boots of Jed O'Brien. No one could.

When the next farmstead over had come up for sale, and with Jamie and his wife, Lauren, living just two miles down the road, it was too good of an opportunity to let slide.

Plus, it gave Trey a chance to work doing what he loved, restoring old homes. He liked the idea of taking something most people would pass by and turning it into something beautiful.

The gravel rocks under his tires ground out a familiar sound as he pulled into the driveway and parked at the guesthouse. A warmth settled in his chest as he sat for a second, taking a deep breath and enjoying the serenity home gave him. Yes, he owned a house he loved, but this land, these buildings...this would always be what his heart recognized as home.

The guesthouse sat across from the main house, positioned at the edge of the property tucked into a grove of trees. A slightly sloped backyard gave way to a lazy creek where Trey and Jamie still enjoyed throwing in a fishing line from time to time.

Trey loved the guesthouse and had spent countless hours there as a teenager. It had been nothing but an old work cabin when his father had given him the keys.

"It's all ours as long as you work extra for the supplies. And I'd like to know your plans for the place before you make any changes," Jed had said as he handed his youngest the keys.

After that, any extra time Trey could find was spent reworking the old space. He'd torn down walls and added more. He knew the supplies always available to him outweighed the extra amount of time he spent shoveling pig shit or mowing lawns. Still, every Sunday afternoon when church was over and their stomachs were full, Jed would slap a hand on Trey's shoulder and say, "Well, what work do you have for me today?"

Working on the guesthouse with his Dad and brother every Sunday became the highlight of his week. Yes, chasing girls, bonfires with his friends, and throwing around the football on Friday nights was great, but in his mind, nothing would ever compare to the Sunday afternoons he spent with a hammer in his hand and his family by his side.

Eve waved toward her son and a broad smile stretched across her face as she walked out to greet him.

"Where've you been? You missed Saturday morning breakfast," she scolded, lightly hitting his chest as he leaned in to kiss her cheek.

Keeping his hands on her shoulders, he took a step back and leaned down to make himself eye level with his petite mom. With a smile on his face and silliness in his voice that had been getting him out of trouble since he was fifteen, he teased, "Mama, I am a grown-ass man. Believe me," he winked at her, "you do not want to know where I've been."

Eve feigned offense at his cockiness, but she knew all too well the type of trouble her youngest often found. This town and the surrounding ones were too small to avoid the rumors that circulated about her boys.

"Goodness, Trey." She huffed and rolled her eyes. "Will you ever grow up?" Trey slid his arm around her shoulder, pulling her against him and laughing as they walked toward the house.

"Why the hell would I want to do that?"

His mother shook her head. "When will you find your 'Lauren'?"

As if on cue, Jamie walked out onto the wrap around porch of their family home. Eve and Trey stopped their conversation, watching the familiar sight play out before them.

Jamie held onto the beauty who had owned him since his sophomore year in high school. Pulling his wife, Lauren, to his chest, she giggled and stood on her tiptoes to lay a quick kiss on his lips. She turned away from him, trying to get back into the house.

"Girl, where do you think you're going? You come back here and give your man a proper kiss." He reached out and snatched her around the waist. Lauren let out a yelp and began playfully slapping at Jamie's biceps in a weak attempt to get him to let go.

"Stop, Jamie! I need to get those dishes done so Alex and I can get to Mommy and Me Hour at the library."

Jamie knew how this worked. He'd been playing this game with his girl since long before Alex was born. He nuzzled into his wife's neck, loving how she acted like she didn't have time for him, but knowing exactly what it did to her when he kissed this spot.

"Alex, baby!" Jamie yelled out, knowing his daughter was sitting on the other side of the screen door watching cartoons, "Tell your Mama to give me a kiss or I will tickle her until she gives in."

Without missing a beat, Alex O'Brien yelled out, "Better do it, Mama! Did I tell you he tickled me until I peed last time?"

Lauren gasped and Jamie froze, his eyes bulging. She looked up at her husband and shook her head. "You didn't," she whispered as she leaned into him.

Jamie smiled down at the love of his life. He thought he wouldn't want her any more than the day they were married, but then she had given him the perfect gift. The sassy four-year-old with blonde hair and brown eyes who had just ratted him out about the "pee incident" even after he had bribed her with not one, but two suckers.

Man, his girls were a handful, but he wouldn't have it any other way.

Alex was not only the mirror image of her beautiful

mother but also the person who had breathed life back into this entire family after his father's death.

Jamie nodded as he pulled his wife closer and said, "I did."

Trey leaned over and whispered in his Mom's ear, "Not everyone gets a Lauren, Mama." He kissed the top of her head and released her as he walked ahead.

"Okay, okay. Enough with the mushing," Trey yelled. His brother reluctantly moved away from his wife but wrapped a protective arm around her waist. Trey wondered for just a second what it must feel like to have two people you felt such responsibility for. Sure, he loved his family and would do anything for them, but he knew it couldn't possibly compare to the feelings Jamie had for Lauren and Alex.

"Well, well. Look who decided to show up for work today," Jamie teased. "Rough night?"

Trey gave his brother a full-on smile, raising his eyebrows and laughing under his breath but loud enough for everyone to hear, "Not nearly as rough as I like it, Bro."

"Oh, for the Love of God, Trey. Please," Eve pleaded as she walked past him.

"And who was the lucky lady this time?" Jamie pressed his brother for information. Trey wasn't usually the kiss and tell type, but he never lied to his brother.

"A Miss Kelsey Jones won the prize last night," he play-fully answered as he removed his ball cap, placed it over his heart and gave a small dip of his head.

Jamie laughed as Lauren crossed her arms over her chest. Smiling she said, "And what prize would that be? The STD of the month?"

Trey opened his mouth and gasped, but he couldn't hide the smirk, "Sis! Words hurt! No wonder my niece is..."

Before he could finish his sentence with the words, "full of sass," his favorite voice in the whole world yelled, "Uncle Trey!"

A bundle of blonde curls with the energy of a squirrel on crack came busting out of the screen door and didn't stop. Alex launched herself off the steps and into the waiting arms of her uncle.

"Whoa there, Firefly!" he laughed as he spun her in a circle. He'd called her that since the day she came home from the hospital. When she was born, her blood work had been high on some numbers, or low, he wasn't sure. Trey could never remember what, but the doctors had sent her home with a blanket that glowed and was supposed to help with whatever it was she needed.

She had been his little firefly from that moment.

"Guess what?! Guess what?!" She bounced around in his arms and he knew exactly what she was going to say.

"Hmm, let me see. You're going to tell me you ate all of your green beans at supper last night."

She paused for only a second. "Yucky, no! I want to tell you ..." He put his hand up in front of her face. She hated when he did that, so she swatted it away.

"No, no, wait. I want to guess. I bet you're going to tell me your daddy is a big, fat booger-eater because he is, you know? From way back!"

"Nooo," she drew out the word in the most dramatic fashion that only a four-year-old could do. "Uncle Trey, that's not it!"

"Well, what could be more important, little Firefly?" He tapped his finger against his cheek, looking to the sky like the answer was written in the clouds.

She threw her hands above her head, ready to deliver the most fantastic news. "Tomorrow is my birthday!"

Trey furrowed his eyebrows and gave his niece a stern look. "No, no, that's not right. Nope, tomorrow is not your birthday because you're not allowed to get any bigger."

"I'm already getting bigger. See?" She lifted her tiny arms and scrunched her face together, trying as hard as she could to make an impression. "See my muscles?"

"Geesh, I guess you are getting big." He squeezed one of her little arms like he was testing her strength. "Has your dad been making you throw around hay bales in the barn?"

"Nope, it's just what happens when you get big. And guess what again?"

"I don't know if I can take anymore, Firefly," Trey said as he buried his face in her neck, acting like he wanted to take a big bite and getting the exact laughing and kicking response he was looking for.

Between giggles and screams, she yelled out, "I have a boyfriend!"

All things stopped.

He pulled away from his niece and laid a hard stare over her shoulder and right at his brother. "I'm sorry, what did you say?"

Alex laid a small hand on either side of her uncle's face, forcing him to make eye contact with her.

"I said I have a boyfriend and I love him." Her little eyes searched his face, wanting to make sure he understood her. Trey faintly registered the laughing coming from his family.

He did not think it was funny.

"No, you don't," Trey said.

"I do, too. We even sit by each other at the library. Tell him, Mama."

Trey pointed his finger at his sister-in-law as she laughed and hid behind her husband, "Don't you say a word, Lauren. Not one word."

He softened his voice, looking at his niece. "Now listen, baby. You don't need a boyfriend. Your Daddy and me, we are all you will ever need. We love you way more than any old, stinky boy could."

Alex drew in a deep breath, lifted her shoulders to her ears and whispered, "But Collin is so cute."

"Cute? Cute, is he? No way he's cuter than your Uncle Trey. And what kind of name is Collin?"

He looked over his niece's head at her parents. "Collin who?"

"Trey," Lauren said softly, "now just calm down."

"Collin who?" he asked again.

His brother kicked at something invisible with his boot, not wanting to make eye contact. "Collin Baker."

"What?! As in Adam Baker's kid? He's like, what...six or seven?" He looked back at his niece. "Is he seven? He's too old for you, Firefly."

"Trey calm down," his brother said.

"Adam Baker is a prick and you know it."

"Swear word," Alex announced.

Trey lowered his niece to the ground, digging in his pocket until he found a five-dollar bill to pay his fee for swearing in front of her. "Sorry, Firefly." He mumbled as he absentmindedly handed it to her outstretched hand.

"Why don't you and Grandma go check on those newborn kittens we saw in the barn last weekend. Uncle Trey will be there in a few minutes."

She shrugged her shoulders, smiling at her new-found wealth. "Okay," she quickly agreed as she grabbed her Grandmother's hand.

Alex motioned to Eve, encouraging her to bend down to her level and then stated matter-of-factly, "He took it better than I thought." Eve threw her head back and laughed as they turned toward the barn. "I'm sure it won't be the last you hear of it, Sweetie."

"Wait!" Alex blurted. She spun around and sprinted toward her uncle. He squatted down opening his arms to her. She threw her arms around his neck and squeezed with all her four, almost five, year-old might.

"Don't worry, I will always love you and Daddy more," she whispered.

TWO

Trey watched his niece bounce up and down, dragging her grandmother along as they headed toward the barn. Something inside told him he might never find his Lauren, but he was okay with that because there was a confident little girl who already owned his heart.

And speaking of that, he turned to face Jamie and Lauren who were still standing on the porch.

He rested his hands on his hips and pursed his lips together.

Jamie lifted his hands up in defense as his brother closed the distance between them. "Now hold on a minute, let's talk about it," he laughed.

Trey marched up the wooden steps as he shook his head. "Talk about what? Maybe how you two are royally screwing up this parenting thing?"

Lauren laughed and swung the dishtowel she'd been holding onto in Trey's direction.

Trey pointed at her, "You get a pass because you're so cute and my niece looks like you." He swung his arm over her shoulder, giving her a quick, brotherly kiss on the side of her head and led her back toward the kitchen door. He changed his voice as if he were talking to a child, "Plus, you've already proven you're not the most intelligent person by marrying my brother."

She shoved him, but he spun around to face them, walking backward toward the door as he pointed at his brother, "But you, you are just a horrible father! And as soon as I'm done kicking Adam Baker's ass, I'm coming for you!"

Jamie lunged at his younger brother just as Trey threw open the door and ran into the kitchen. "What does a guy have to do to get some breakfast around here?" He yelled into the empty house as the door slammed behind him.

"You need to make it your damn self since you were so late," Lauren yelled back as her husband grabbed the door and held it open for her.

Trey was already waist deep in the refrigerator by the time Jamie and Lauren joined him.

"One more thing, on a serious note," Lauren said to Trey's backside, "Please don't forget to pick up the cupcakes for tomorrow."

Trey spun around, standing as straight as he could, eyes looking forward, "Yes, Ma'am. I mean, no, Ma'am. I will not let you down. At exactly eleven a.m., I will retrieve my niece's birthday cupcakes from the bakery, decorated in half Frozen and half Ironman," he risked a glance down at Lauren and whispered, "because she is the most awesome girl ever." He straightened back up again, mimicking a soldier standing at attention, "And I will deliver said cupcakes directly to this farm to be eaten by a bunch of crazy animals in little kid suits."

She gently patted his chest as she walked passed him, "You're so strange."

Jamie smirked at his brother. "One of these days she's going to lay you out."

Trey slid a plateful of cold cuts, leftover from yesterday's lunch, onto the table and turned to grab a gallon of milk. He shoved a piece of cheese into his mouth, looking at his brother like he was nuts as he slammed the refrigerator door. "No way, she loves me. Grab the bread for me, will you?"

Jamie turned and grabbed a loaf of their mama's homemade bread from the bread box and slid it in front of his brother.

Trey's eyes twinkled with mischief as he grabbed the package. "Why don't you go out with Andy and me tonight? Just come out and have a couple of beers. You can leave before any of the fun starts."

Jamie shook his head, "Are you crazy? Lauren would have my balls on a plate if I even thought about going out the night before Alex's birthday party." Trey laughed and went to work making a man-sized sandwich. He knew before he even asked there was no way his brother would go and would've probably kicked his ass himself if he tried, but sometimes he liked to have ammunition for future insults. Not being able to go out with the guys because your wife won't let you is classic stuff.

"Where are you guys going? Are you staying here in town?"

"Just over to Huntsville. They have a live band playing and I'm hoping to catch up with Kelsey again. She was..." he stopped for a second and smiled to himself, remembering all the trouble she had let him get into last night, "fun." Trey laughed at his own joke but was hoping he would run into her. Last night had been the first time he'd ever seen her and he liked the challenge of someone who wasn't from around here.

After a few minutes, Trey realized the weight of the silence in the room.

Jamie was leaned up against the counter, arms crossed over his chest, one booted foot crossed over the other.

Trey looked around the room, confused and wondering what he had done to get the "Dad stare" from his brother. "What?' What did I do?"

His brother cleared his throat and ran his hand down his face. "Look, Mom and Lauren are worried about you."

Trey sat up straighter in his seat, the last bite of his sandwich hanging halfway out of his mouth. "Me? Why the hell are they worried about me? I'm fine."

"Maybe we're worried because all you seem to do is hang out with sleazy women in dive bars and drink until you can't remember where you are," Lauren added as she walked back into the room.

Trey raised his arms out to the side and lifted his shoulders to his ears, sandwich in one hand, a glass of milk in the other. "Yes...and? I'm still waiting for the part you should be worried about."

Jamie shook his head. "I think what my lovely wife is trying to say is, they are worried because you don't show any signs of slowing down. They, Mom and Lauren, think maybe your drinking is getting out of hand."

Trey's chair screeched as he stood. "So, you think I'm a drunk."

"No," both Lauren and Jamie said in unison.

"So, you think I'm a loser?"

"No," Lauren said again. Jamie tipped his head to the side, lifting his eyebrows like Trey might be on to something.

Trey punched him in the chest.

"Ouch, Dickhead. No, I don't think you're a loser, but I do want you to be careful. You have no idea what these girls want from you."

Trey let out a sarcastic laugh, "I know exactly what these girls want."

"Stop with the joking, Trey. We're serious. Don't you ever think about finding a nice girl and settling down?" Lauren looked down at the dishtowel she had twisted into a ball.

Trey picked up the plate of meat and covered it back up, turning to put it back in the refrigerator and escape the seriousness of the moment.

"Of course, but right now, I don't know. Maybe it's just not in the cards for me." He shoved the plate back from where he had gotten it and turned to see the caring, almost sad look in his sister-in-law's eyes.

"We just don't want you to be alone."

"I know and I'm not. I have you two and my little Firefly and Mom. You're all I need right now. Not everyone can find their true love at age fifteen. I'm only twenty-four and have a lot of time to find someone. When I'm ready, I'll find my Mrs. Forever, but right now...I just want to find my Miss Whatever."

Lauren threw her head back, growled into the air and tossed the dishtowel into the sink. "You are impossible. You know that?"

Trey flashed his famous 1000-watt smile. "I do, sweet sister, and that's exactly why it's better for me to be single. I would drive some poor girl crazy with all my antics."

"That's the first bit of sense I've heard from you today." She admitted as she hugged her brother-in-law. "Please be careful," she whispered as she turned away from the O'Brien brothers and stepped out onto the porch.

Lauren knew exactly how lucky she had been when Jamie had fallen for her in high school. Her family life had been less than stellar with a dad who hadn't stuck around and a mother who was more interested in her latest bar fling than the little girl who was home alone, making herself supper, and putting herself to bed.

But Jamie had saved her from all that. There was nothing comparable to the love of an O'Brien boy. Once Jamie introduced her to his family, she was theirs. No questions asked.

The O'Brien's had everything a girl would want. Spitting images of their dad and each other, they stood a head taller than most of the men in town. Sandy brown hair and tanned skin from working outside made them look more like surfers than farmers, but one look at their hands and you knew these men were no slackers.

But beyond that, there was a presence the O'Brien men carried with them. It wasn't arrogance and it certainly wasn't because they thought of themselves as better than anyone else. It was the understanding they had to work hard for everything. They worked hard on the farm, worked hard for each other and worked hard in their relationships. If something wasn't functioning correctly, they worked until they fixed it. There was power in knowing no matter what happened, your family was always standing next to you, fighting with you every step of the way.

To every girl in a fifty-mile radius, Trey was the man to get. He had money, looks and security. There wasn't a week that went by when some gold-digging bitch didn't buddy up to her at the library, grocery store, or local swimming pool, asking about her handsome brother-in-law. It made her sick to think he might be tricked into a relationship with someone who was only looking to attach herself to the O'Brien name.

All you needed to do was spend five seconds with Trey and his niece to see the way into his heart. If he got some random girl pregnant, it would all be over. He would marry her without so much as a second thought.

Back in the kitchen, Trey turned to his brother after watching Lauren walk out of the room. "What's going on with her?" He asked.

His big brother grabbed an apple from the counter and took a bite, staring at the apple in his hand while chewing and choosing his next words carefully.

"We think maybe you're running too hard and too fast."

"What the hell does that mean?"

"Well, you never just...pause."

"Pause?" Trey questioned.

Jamie set the half-eaten apple down and pushed himself off the counter. "Yeah, pause. Lauren reminds me all the time that I need to stop barreling through life. We do that, you know? You and me, we get our minds set on one thing and we don't stop until it's done."

Trey understood exactly what his brother meant. They'd been raised to believe there was nothing too big or too much or too hard for an O'Brien. They kept pushing forward until it was no longer an obstacle.

"She says we are always so hell-bent on what task is in front of us, we forget life is happening around us. We forget to pause and be thankful for what we have. We get so head-strong about building our lives we forget to live life. The pause is so we don't miss the little things. The important things. The experiences that make up the memories of someone's life."

A comfortable silence stretched out between them as Trey pondered everything his brother was saying. He let out a low whistle as he slowly nodded his head, "Jesus, that wife of yours is something else. You are one lucky man."

"You don't have to tell me, brother. I already know. Anyway, she's worried if you don't learn to pause, you're going to miss all the good things that are happening and possibly, miss the one woman who is meant to be yours. There's a woman made just for you and she's out there right now. God help her."

Trey let out a small, soft laugh. He dropped a calloused hand onto his brother's shoulder, squeezing it a little to show how much he appreciated him. Looking him in the eye, he took a deep breath. "Okay. I promise I will pause more often. I don't want to miss any of this. And I would never forgive myself if I missed my opportunity to have the life you guys have."

Jamie smiled, nodding his head. "Good. That's really good, Trey."

Trey slammed his other hand down on his brother's shoulder and tried to shake him forcefully, "But can I please wait to pause until tomorrow? Because I really want some more of Miss Kelsey tonight!"

Trey walked across the kitchen and out the door onto the porch where his sister-in-law sat in a rocking chair.

He turned toward his brother who had followed him outside. "I'm going to go check on the far west fence line." He grabbed the bill of his cap, squeezed it, and pulled it farther down on his head.

"Sounds good. Let me know if you need help."

Trey bounced down the steps before turning back toward the house and pointing with both hands toward Lauren and Jamie. "I'm giving you guys two days to straighten out this boyfriend mess with my niece. If the boyfriend is not gone, I will have no choice but to take matters into my own hands."

Lauren watched as Trey walked backward away from them. "What are you going to do, threaten a seven-year-old boy?"

"You don't worry about it. You guys should go read some parenting books or something. What to expect or some shit like that."

"Those are pregnancy books, you idiot," Lauren chuckled.

"Well, it looks like you guys might be in real trouble here. Wouldn't be a bad idea to go back, way back, like to conception."

Jamie threw up his middle finger in his brother's direction.

Trey shook his head, laughing at the gesture. "I'm off to own that broken fence. Nothing will stop me today." He turned toward his truck and pointed one finger to the sky, about to claim his success over the day that had just started, "I'm an O'Brien and I'm going to..."

"Uncle Trey!" He stopped in his tracks when he heard the small voice coming from the barn.

"go look at baby kittens," he finished as he quickly turned away from his truck and started toward his niece. "That's what I'm going to do. Kiss baby kittens with my little Firefly. Then, I will own that fence." He said, running toward the barn.

"Cupcakes! Eleven...in the morning, Trey. Eleven in the morning!" Lauren yelled after him.

He lifted his hand above his head, giving Lauren an okay and silently praying he didn't forget those damn cupcakes.

8:30 PM

Text message:

Jamie: Cupcakes are ready early, so if u want to pick them up before 11 go for it.

Trey: I've been so worried.

Jamie: Dickhead. U out yet?

Trey: Nope. Just waiting for Andy. Last chance, sure u don't want to join us?

Jamie: 100% sure, dude. Have fun, good luck finding Miss STD, I mean Miss Jones.

Trey: Hey, don't talk about the future Mrs. Trey O'Brien like that

Jamie: haha .. my bad

11:00 PM

Trey: U still up?

Jamie: Nope

Trey: I may have a problem

Jamie: What's new

Trey: Seems Miss Jones was actually Mrs. Jones

Jamie: Oh shit

Trey: Word has it Mr. Jones is not happy with me

Jamie: You're an idiot

Trey: I know

Jamie: Need me to pick you up?

Trey: And deal with Lauren's wrath all day tomorrow, no thanks. I'll find Andy and call it a night.

Jamie: Lauren says you're an idiot too.

Trey: I think you guys might be onto something. See you in the morning.

12:45 AM

Jamie frantically reached into the dark for his phone, hoping to answer it before his wife woke up.

"Hello," he whispered, trying to slip out of bed. He stopped when Lauren flipped on the nightstand lamp.

"Is he okay?" she asked her husband, rubbing the sleep from her eyes.

"I don't know yet, baby."

"Are you okay?" he asked into the phone.

There was silence on the other end. "Trey, you there?"

Jamie waited only a few seconds before standing and yelling into the phone, "Trey!"

His brother's voice was hushed. The sound made the hair on the back of his neck stand up.

"Jamie, I'm in real trouble."

Jamie reached for his pants and shoes as Lauren jumped out of bed, scrambling to hand him his shirt.

"I'm coming. Where are you, what's wrong?"

"I'm in the back room of The Flamingo. It's in Huntsville."

"What the hell is going on?" Lauren asks as she handed her husband his wallet and keys to his truck.

"He's in some storage room in a bar in Huntsville."

"What? Why?"

"What exactly is going on, Trey?"

"Her husband showed up and brought a bunch of guys with him. I can't find Andy anywhere and brother, these guys aren't here to talk."

"Okay, just stay there and stay out of sight. I'll text you when I'm in the alley. Come out the back door and I'll be waiting for you."

"Tell him to call the police, Jamie." Lauren raised her voice in hopes her brother-in-law would hear her through the line. "Trey, just call the damn police and stay where you are. Don't do anything stupid."

"Jamie," Trey whispered.

"Yeah?"

"Hurry."

"I'm already in my truck."

1:15 AM

911 Call:

"911, what is your emergency?"

"Hurry, please! Oh my God, hurry, damn it!! There's blood everywhere!"

"Sir, who is hurt?"

"It's my brother... he's bleeding, it's his blood... his blood is everywhere! Please! Someone stabbed my brother!"

"Where are you?"

"NO!! No, you don't! Keep your damn eyes open! Don't you die! Please hurry, he's dying!! We're in the alley behind The Flamingo!"

"Okay, we have units on the way. Stay on the phone with me. Sir? Sir, can you talk to me?"

"Someone... anyone, please! Please help us!"

"Sir? Sir are you still with me?"

"Yes, please hurry...he's dying!"

"Tell me your brother's name. "

"Sir, are you there? Can you tell me your brother's name?"

"There's so much blood."

"Do you know CPR? I can talk you through CPR. Sir!"

"I think he's gone."

"Stay on the phone with me. I can help. What is your brother's name?"

"His name...his name is Jamie O'Brien."

THREE

CALLIE LOFTIER STOOD ANKLE DEEP IN THE ATLANTIC. The clouded skies released a soft mist, rinsing away all the tension she held in her body. With her eyes closed, she turned her face toward the sky and offered up a small smile along with all the worries she'd carried for what seemed to be an eternity.

She'd been shackled in the darkness of her illness for so long, she couldn't even imagine being free of it. But here, as she listened to the tide rush and pull against itself, she felt a quickening in her soul. It felt wild and alive, and she welcomed it with everything she had.

The waves rose up in the distance, sounding out a slow crescendo as their rolling rhythm continued toward her. The chaos around her swirled to a perfect combination of beautiful confusion. She loved the idea of giving up control to something so demanding.

Everything in her life had always been careful, planned out...sterile.

But today she stood on the edge of so many uncertainties. A small shiver crawled up her back as she listened to the world happening around her. Her shoulders rose and fell as she took a resolving breath and wished things had been different. It wasn't regret, not really, just a fleeting thought.

Soft tears fell freely from her eyes. They weren't sad tears. These were the type that didn't ask permission but trailed down your cheeks anyway. She felt zero attachment to them. They were happening because she should be feeling something. There should be something churning inside her, something that pushed her to change her mind, but she felt completely at peace.

Hope had a stinging effect when you hang all your possibilities on it. She had turned off the bite of that emotion long ago to merely survive. These tears were her heart's way of offering up an apology to the universe for her lack of self-preservation.

She wiped them from her cheeks as soon as they fell and took a step into the water.

Concentrating on the movement of sand under her feet, she stood frozen. Every small wave that rushed past her ankles brought new sand toward her. It rushed up and over her feet, burying them under thousands of pebbles. But just as quickly, the water would recede, stealing sand from underneath her feet and pulling it back into the water. She opened her eyes and watched as the ocean went from covering her and burying her deeply in the sand, to quickly exposing her all over again.

She felt the familiar burn in her lungs that happened when she was off her oxygen for too long. Her chest rose and fell more rapidly than it should have to, trying so hard to keep her levels high enough.

For twenty-one years, her body had fought this race

against time and for a while, even when she knew her body was losing the battle, her mind refused to accept it.

But time wore on and she continued to grow more fragile each day. "After you get better," became nothing more than words. It was no longer a real-time in her mind like it had been before.

She acted as if she had plans for the future, as if she still believed in the fairytale of a healthy life. Not for herself, but for her parents and her sister, Jade. False promises and fake intentions had been the stones that paved this journey for so long now. She wasn't sure she knew any other way.

It was funny how lies became acceptable if told under the intention of sheltering the ones you loved from the pain of the truth.

Her entire life people had called her a fighter, but for the last year and a half, the only thing she had honestly been was tired.

Tired of being strong. Tired of being sick. And mostly, tired of living life like everything was going to be okay.

It was the going to be that weighed the heaviest on her.

The going to be okay, the going to be better, and the going to be different when. A life built on those words could never really be considered a life at all. One of her hardest days was when she realized while she sat in a hospital bed waiting for the "going to be" to happen, life was going on without her.

Nothing could take away the hurt of a lost future. Callie wanted to scream at the top of her lungs, wanted her family to see she was already gone. Then maybe this wouldn't hurt them as much. Wasn't there some way to let them know they loved her the best they could?

If love were enough, she wouldn't have been sick. If love

were enough, none of them would've had to suffer through her cursed life.

There had always been a goodbye meant for them and if she could, she would fight longer for them. But her fate was already written in the stars. She had to love them enough to say goodbye and release them from all of this.

Physically her illness made it impossible to get out of bed some days, and other days there was nothing to get out of bed for. Emotionally, she was already dead. She spent most of her time confined to her parents' beach house, only experiencing things through the windows. She'd never been to a dance, never spent a night out with her friends, never even been in love.

But today was different. Today, Callie left all of that behind and would finally be free. She breathed as deeply as she could, trying to fill her soul with the peace she had at this very moment. If there was one thing she hoped she could take with her, it was this feeling.

The sounds of the beach, the lapping of the water against her ankles...this is how she'd always pictured it. Callie looked out onto the water that stretched well beyond what she could see and welcomed the feeling of insignificance. There was no more room in her life for selfishness, no more longing for something never meant to be hers. She was such a small part of the universe, meant to be overlooked and forgotten. And it was okay. A small smile stretched across her lips as she realized...it really was okay.

She moved deeper into the water. It splashed up a bit higher on her legs making her sway a little more, her muscles tensing against the push and pull force. Her breaths quickened, trying to keep up with the small increase in energy demand needed to keep her upright.

There was no promise of tomorrow for her. She knew

this. She knew every tomorrow that came would only hold the disappointment of another day gone by while she remained stagnant. There was no moving forward. The only changes ever made were in the wrong direction. She couldn't bear it any longer. She had tamed her last personal demon, healed her last disappointment.

Her parents and sister were heavy on her overworked heart. Even if the miracle they prayed for happened, she would never be normal, never feel like everyone else. She would forever be a captive of her unforgiving memories. There would always be the fear of death looming over her like it had since she was old enough to understand she was living on borrowed time.

She took another step forward, her fingertips barely dipping into the water. She watched as the waves built up and rolled in her direction. She wondered for a second what it would have been like to live a normal life but stopped herself. She had gone down that road so many times. She'd cried the tears, felt the pain, and had let it go.

A wave rolled up unexpectedly, pushing her to the side and she stumbled. Her breaths were coming one after another as her heart beat painfully fast and hard in her chest.

She took another step.

The burning in her chest intensified and her vision darkened around the edges. She swayed with the direction of the water, a slave to the tide. Callie looked to the sky once again as the tips of her toes skimmed along the sandy ocean floor. Watching as the birds circled, she hoped it would be like that. She wanted to feel the freedom of the breeze on her face and have the world finally unfold in front of her with no restrictions.

She exhaled as a wave rushed toward her, took one more step, and let go of everything.

JADE RAN FROM HER PARENTS' house after hearing the commotion coming from the beach. She took the stone steps that led from the patio onto the sand two at a time as her mom's screams cut through the early morning light.

She hit the sand running as she watched her dad plow through the water toward her sister. What was Callie doing out here? How did she even make it that far on her own? Reality ripped through her causing her to stumble as she realized what was happening.

Everything began to spin as fear shot through her veins. "No...no. No! NO!"

Her mom fell to her knees in the sand sobbing into her hands as Jade ran to the water's edge, searching the horizon for any sign of them.

Jade dropped to her knees, closing her arms around her mom. This couldn't be happening. Callie didn't even know this was the day they had all been waiting on. The day all their prayers had been answered.

FOUR

TWO YEARS LATER

THE RAIN FELL IN FAT DROPLETS ONTO CALLIE'S windshield. Color spread into running kaleidoscopes down the glass as it reflected the headlights stretching out onto the blacktopped road.

She hadn't seen another car for twenty miles leading into the last small town and didn't expect to see any now that she was ten miles on the other side of it. Two o'clock in the morning was the time of lovers and seekers, not regular people just out for a drive.

Lightning flashed in front of her chasing itself across the dark sky. For a split second, she saw her own eyes in the rearview mirror and quickly looked away.

A rumbling began in the distance and rushed toward her, shaking the ground and engulfing everything in its path causing a shiver to crawl up her spine. She smiled. She should be anxious and maybe even a bit afraid, but she loved the rain too much to disrespect it like that.

The first thing she'd done after waking up from surgery

was made several promises to herself. Worry, anxiety, and regret were silly emotions. She no longer had time for them.

The universe didn't give second chances at life often. She wouldn't use it foolishly.

A purple lightning streak raced across the sky once again, cutting through the blackness in a dramatic light show. It called to Callie, igniting her need for freedom.

She pulled her car to the side of the road and stepped out into the night's storm as she made her way into the middle of the road. Stretching her arms out to the side, she closed her eyes and lifted her face to the sky. The rain dampened her simple cotton shift dress. It clung to her thin frame as she turned in slow circles. The shower was rejuvenating, and it left her wondering why she had never revisited the water. It wasn't the ocean that had meant her harm.

Callie didn't ask the rain where it came from or why it was here. She didn't curse it or wonder how long it would stay. She just allowed it to kiss her body and bless her into this new life. Never again would she question the moments of her life. Her goal was to live in every second and feel every emotion. Allow all situations to happen as they were supposed to, uninterrupted and raw.

The thunderstorm played out its medley as she turned and swayed back and forth in time to the raindrops hitting the pavement.

Screeching tires cut through the night, disrupting Callie's love affair with the rain. She turned toward the noise, dropping her arms and taking a few quick steps to the side as her breathing jumped to a hurried pace. Her curiosity piqued. Who else would be in the middle of nowhere at this time of night?

The rain continued, demanding her attention and running in streams down her face as her heart beat steady and sure in her chest. Her breaths echoed in her ears, mixing with the roar of the truck's engine. She struggled to look beyond the glaring headlights.

The sky lit up, briefly cutting through the darkness of the truck's cab, giving her only a second's look at the driver. His hands gripped the top of the steering wheel tightly while wild eyes strained to focus on her. Anger and confusion flashed across his face before being swallowed back into the darkness.

Callie was motionless as she stared into the cab. All her life she had feared the dark, scared of the unknown, but tonight her spirit was at ease.

She felt the weight of his eyes on her. She relaxed her shoulders, tilting her head to the side. Callie had a different understanding of life now and realized nothing happened without purpose. People came into your life for a reason and situations happened because they were supposed to. This was the exact type of human experience she had been cheated out of before and craved so badly.

Callie wondered who would be changed by this night. Was this chance meeting a part of his story or her own?

The wind stirred through the grassy ditches toward her, lifting the hem of her dress slightly and changing the rain's direction. She filled her lungs with a long, full breath.

Once again, the sky lit up and she could see him. He'd shifted forward, resting his chin on his hands, watching her. It was just the two of them and the alluring rain. She smiled as a wave of shyness passed through her and she dropped her eyes to the ground.

In the distance, another round of thunder began like an invitation. She was unprepared for the cry of the stars and the moon, but somehow it felt right like it was calling her home. Callie returned to the rain, giving it all her attention. She ran her hands up the sides of her face as she lifted her arms above her head and turned away from the man in the truck. Even standing in the chilly rain, her body felt on fire.

Through the roaring storm, Callie heard the truck door open.

He was hesitant at first, toying with the idea of joining her. He lingered for a moment, half in her world, half in his safety.

Callie closed her eyes, swaying to the song of the rain.

His boots hit the pavement, closing the distance between them, and she felt every step he made toward her like a rushing in her soul.

"This is dangerous," she thought to herself, a flash of her old life rearing its head. But she stopped the fears quickly.

"No, this is living," she corrected.

She wanted to feel everything, live in all the moments without the fear she had lived with for too long. Maybe it was reckless or silly, but she didn't care.

He stepped up behind her, and she felt his rushed breaths in her hair.

This dance was for him.

The rain hit the pavement, jumping around her ankles. The wind twisted through and around them, licking at their wet skin and urging them on.

Timid fingertips touched her bare arm and a million silent questions were asked. Callie stilled. They were here, in this moment...together. His hand traveled down her arm, his large calloused fingers skimming her skin, searching until her fingers intertwined with his. She pulled his thick arm around her waist.

A thunderous boom rang out, startling her. She jumped, covering her mouth as his other arm slid possessively around her waist. "I've got you," he whispered as his warm breath bathed across the soft skin behind her ear.

His hand spread out over her stomach, and for just a second, she thought he might step away. Instead, he gently pulled her in.

"And I've got you," she whispered. She relaxed against him, feeling the strong planes of his chest against her back. He wrapped his body around hers, protecting her, holding her. His wet lips pressed lightly to her neck as raindrops rolled off his hair and down onto her shoulder. She ran her hand down his arm and started to sway again, inviting him into her dance.

They danced together in the spotlight of his truck lights and their show was beautiful. Callie squeezed his hands, pulling him closer as he nuzzled into her, inhaling deeply like he wanted this to be his last breath. He released one of her hands, softly running his fingertips up her arm and she stopped moving, melting even further into him. She wanted to remember every inch of his skin on hers.

He leaned to her ear once again, squeezed her tightly and just as quickly as he was there, he was gone.

She gasped at his sudden absence and turned back toward him, gripping the fabric of her dress where his hands had just been over her stomach. A small tremor took over and her stomach knotted as she watched him walk away from their moment...away from her.

He pushed one hand into his front pocket as he reached up and grabbed the back of his neck with the other.

Knowing the cab light would turn on when he opened the door, Callie turned away. Seeing him would only make it harder. She wanted her heart to remember this, not her mind.

The gravel shifted under his tires as he slowly drove

around her on the side shoulder of the road. She watched until his tail lights were gone.

"That was definitely for me," she whispered into the night, running a finger lightly over her scar. She looked up at the stars that had just started to peek through the clouds. "Thank you."

CALLIE PULLED into the driveway and parked in front of the large farmhouse. She dropped her head back against the headrest.

She was ready, but she silently prayed the timing was right for everyone else, too.

She wrapped her sweater around her shoulders and ran up the steps, not sure if it was her, or if the temperature had dropped several degrees, but she was suddenly cold. Soaked from head to toe, she stood in front of the wooden door. She crossed her arms in front of her chest, trying to hold onto everything she had become to get her to this moment. Her teeth chattered as she ran her hands up and down her arms.

Reaching out a small, shaking finger, she pushed the doorbell.

"Just a moment," a soft voice called out as the deadbolt unlocked. Callie's flight or fight kicked in and she fought the urge to run back to her car, but the inside door cracked just enough to see the older woman on the other side and everything became crystal clear. She would be sticking around for a while.

"Oh, my goodness. Are you lost, sweetheart?"

Callie looked at the older lady and couldn't stop the smile that spread across her face. "No. I sort of feel like I've finally made it home."

"Excuse me?"

"I know I'm here a few weeks earlier than I thought I would be but, Eve...it's me."

Eve looked closer, studying Callie's face as she gently pushed open the screen door. One hand came up to cover her mouth as she tried to contain a gasp. She reached out toward her and Callie didn't move.

Eve O'Brien slowly moved the neck of Callie's dress to the side, exposing the thick scar on her chest. Her eyes flashed with pain, then filled with tears.

"Callie?"

FIVE

TREY COULDN'T FIGURE OUT WHAT HAD GOTTEN INTO his mom. She'd been hell-bent on him stopping over at the house after work. If there was one thing he knew about Eve O'Brien, when she set her mind to something, she would rearrange the stars in the sky, if need be, to make sure it happens. Even if it meant pulling out the guilt cards.

"Please Trey, it's important," she had begged. And truly, that's all it took.

His chest twisted with guilt as he counted off the months since he'd been to the family farm. Trey knew it was stupid, or stubborn, or maybe even a little cowardly, but didn't care what the reason was behind it. He clenched the steering wheel, wishing like hell he could keep driving and pretend he'd never spoken to his mom today. But she had said it was important and if it was important to her, then it should be important to him. The space he had put between his family and him stung every day. He felt their absence in everything he did, but it was just one more thing he surrendered to his unraveling life.

He called his mom every Friday without fail. Every

other Wednesday, she waited outside the only grocery store in town until she saw him go in and then acted like it was a coincidence they both ended up there. It'd happened a few too many times to be an accident, but he didn't have the heart to call her on it.

On Sunday evenings, she stopped by his place, always with the same excuse - she wanted to see what progress he'd made on his old farmhouse. They both knew it was BS because Trey didn't do that kind of work anymore. He'd done only minor, necessary changes since Jamie's death.

After giving up farming, he'd gone to work for Mr. Gibbons' construction company. He now worked long hours building other people's dreams. Trey's desire to renovate his place had died with Jamie, just like most things in his life.

But it didn't stop Eve from coming over. She bought new curtains for the windows or fresh flowers for his tables. "We need to liven things up a bit in here," she would say while dusting and putting away whatever food she had made him for the week.

She smiled at him, but it never reached her eyes. He didn't hold it against her though. How much can you love someone who was the reason you'd lost so much?

She always made sure he had updated pictures of Alex and Lauren, replacing the old with the new while talking about his niece's upcoming activities. She was trying to keep him connected and he appreciated it, but he never looked at the pictures. All he saw was the life that had been stolen from Jamie.

The life he had stolen.

As soon as his mom left, he'd take the pictures down, hiding them away in the hall closet until the next Sunday, when he would put them out again before Eve arrived. It had become routine, just like her visits.

The wounds he carried about what happened, burned and bled as he watched her move around his house. It made him uncomfortable. Most Sundays he couldn't wait for her to leave. So many times, he'd open his mouth, wanting to talk about the real things. The hard stuff. Pressure would build in his chest as everything that needed to be said sat right below the surface of their fractured relationship.

But he couldn't speak the words out loud, so instead, he thanked her for the food, smiled at the flowers, and hugged her before she left. But it wasn't like before. She was trying to recover from losing Jamie and he was barely surviving. He had nothing left to offer her. His connection to the family was lost, buried under a headstone that read "O'Brien."

So, it wasn't like he had no contact with her, it just wouldn't ever be the same. And he didn't go to the farm... ever. But here he was today, pulling onto the gravel driveway in his work truck. He'd hoped if he showed up right after work, in need of a shower, he could use it as an excuse to leave if things got too uncomfortable.

Nothing had changed as he looked around the familiar farm, except the barn needed painting and by now, his mom's garden was usually in full swing. She had a few things planted but nothing impressive. He didn't want to think about the reasons why she had given up her gardening.

"Oh great," he mumbled to himself as he pulled up to the guesthouse and noticed Andy's truck. Eve had hired Andy, Trey's lifelong best friend, to manage the farm after it was clear Trey wouldn't be taking over. It was a good fit. Andy had been like a son to Eve and Jed and had worked the land as a hired hand since junior high school. He knew how the O'Brien's ran things and had worked countless hours side by side with the brothers.

Still, there was something about it that rubbed Trey the wrong way. He knew he shouldn't have an opinion about who was running things since he'd just up and walked away from it all. However, he couldn't deny how much it bothered him that it was Andy.

Gripping the bill of his old baseball cap with both hands, Trey pulled it down further onto his head. He took a deep breath and closed his eyes for a moment. The best thing for everyone would be for him to pack his bags and move far away from all of them, all of this. But something kept him tethered to this land.

Every night when he laid in his bed replaying that horrible night in the alley, he wondered why it had been Jamie and not him. His death would have been hard for everyone, but not nearly as devastating to the family as losing his brother. Jamie was a husband and a father. He led this family, ran this farm – he was the reason they all stayed together.

With him gone it was different. The absence of him was too significant to ignore. Even though Lauren had told him a million times Jamie's death was not his fault, he could never believe that.

He knew Lauren tolerated him purely out of respect for his brother, but he didn't deserve her forgiveness and if he was honest, he didn't want it. Wanting forgiveness would mean he'd have to be willing to forgive himself and that was something he would never do. If he couldn't bring his brother back, the least he could do was live his life carrying the blame for his death.

Shoving his door open a bit too hard, he jumped out of

the truck. The grass seemed a little too long for his liking. He made a mental note to mention it to Andy. If he was going to be in charge around here, then he damn well better do a good job.

He pushed his hands into his front pockets and headed toward the house. His guts twisted as his anxiety swelled. Every step closer to the house unraveled his already weakened sense of control.

Jamie was all over this place. It was impossible to push away the guilt and shame when everywhere he looked, all he could see was his brother. His forehead glistened with a thin layer of sweat as his breaths rushed in and out too fast.

"Uncle Trey!"

Trey stopped without turning around and swallowed hard against the lump in his throat.

No, not her too. He let out a ragged breath, trying to release some of the pressure building in his chest.

Mustering up the best smile he could, he turned around to face his niece who was running full speed right at him.

"Hey, Firefly." He barely got the words out before she threw her arms around his waist, squeezing with all her might. He patted her small back, tears threatening to fall.

"I can't believe you're here!" Alex squealed as she continued to squeeze her uncle. "Is it really you?"

"It's me alright."

"I haven't seen you for a long time. Don't you miss me, Uncle Trey? 'Cuz I miss you like crazy." Her blue eyes searched his as she looked up adoringly at him.

"Oh, sweet girl," his voice cracked, "I miss you every single day."

He reached down and lifted her into his arms. Burying his face into her hair, he breathed in deeply and selfishly let her embrace make him feel a little better. She'd grown since the last time he had seen her. He held onto her tightly, wishing away all the time lost between the two of them.

She tapped him on the back, "Geesh," she whispered, "you're gonna squeeze the stuffin' out of me."

Trey loosened his grip and lowered the little girl to the ground, kneeling to her level. He pushed away a wild curl and tried tucking it behind her ear.

"You're as beautiful as your Mama, Firefly."

Alex smiled brightly at him, "Yep, I know," she popped her hip out to the side, pointed at her eyes, and blinked dramatically, "but I have my Daddy's eyes."

Trey's heart seized in his chest and his face was suddenly cold as his smile faltered. She did have Jamie's eyes.

He dropped his gaze from her to the ground and twisted his hands together in front of him, trying to stop the tremors that had started.

Alex's hands dropped to her sides. She stood quietly for only a few heartbeats before speaking again.

"Did you know Grandma got me a pony?" She bounced on her toes, hardly able to contain her excitement.

He kept his eyes on the ground but shook his head. He could feel it, the guilt, eating painfully away at him. "No," he finally got out, "no, I didn't know that." He looked up, giving his niece a weak smile.

Alex stopped bouncing and her eyes softened as understanding flashed across her face. He didn't know how, but at that moment he was sure his niece could see into his brokenness. Alex had done a lot of growing up in the last two years and dealt with things no child should.

She wrapped her tiny hands around his, holding onto him tightly.

"Firefly, I..."

His niece cut him off, pulling on his hands. "Well, come and meet her. She is beautiful."

Trey took a deep, long breath as his niece pulled him once more. "Don't be afraid. She is super friendly, and I love her."

"Okay, let's go meet your new pony."

"Yeah!" She shouted as she released his hands and spun in a circle, her arms out to the side. "Her name is Heaven and she is the best pony ever!"

Trey chuckled to himself and watched as Alex ran ahead of him.

He began to follow until a figure stepped out of the shadows of the barn, fixing him to his spot.

He couldn't believe the sight before him. This woman. Trey had thought of nothing but her all night. He'd dreamed of the way her body fit perfectly against his and how it felt when their wet skin touched. Even now, as he stood staring at her, he could hear the soft sounds she made as they swayed in the rain the night before.

And here she was again, standing in front of him, unaware of what her presence was doing to him. Her long blonde hair, which hung freely last night, was now pulled into a thick braid that hung over one shoulder. A few wild strands blew carelessly across her face as she absentmindedly tucked them behind her ear. The same ear he had so gently kissed behind.

The old Def Leppard concert t-shirt she wore hid all her delicious curves outlined in the wet dress she'd worn in the rain the night before. But right this moment, it was the rhythm of her steady breathing – somehow both soft yet compelling – that commanded his attention. She was alive and real, beautifully magnetic in her essence.

She leaned against the open door of the barn, her cut-off

jean shorts barely peeking out past her shirt. One Converse covered foot crossed over the other as she smiled over Alex's head right at him.

He wondered the same thing he had last night as he had watched her in the rain.

Was this a dream?

She glanced at the ground with a shy look. It was the same look she'd given right before she started to dance for him. His entire body reacted to this girl. He wanted to take her into his arms and dance as they had already done. This breathtaking woman lit something within Trey that was both unfamiliar and exciting. A smoldering need to know her sparked inside of him.

Trey's blood suddenly ran cold. He didn't know her or anything about her except for the fact that she was crazy enough to stop in the middle of the road during a thunderstorm to do what, dance? Who does that?

It was suddenly clear who he needed to protect, and it wasn't this girl.

There was something shady about this situation. Who was this girl and why was she here? As much as he wanted it to be true, reality told him it couldn't be a coincidence that she was on the road last night and here now.

What the hell did she want from his family? He knew he had never seen her before their meeting last night, so she'd better have a good reason for standing on his family's land today.

Alex ran past the woman without even a second glance, except for jumping up and giving her a high five. She spun around and yelled back at Trey, "This is my new friend, Callie. She's nice. You will like her, too." And then she was gone, disappearing deeper into the barn.

Callie's smile faltered a bit as she watched his long

strides close the distance between them, noticing the way his thick legs flexed under his jeans. A thin gray t-shirt stretched across his broad chest with the faded marking of what she guessed was his high school mascot. She wound her hands together, trying to ground herself before she burst from anxiety. This impossible situation with an unbelievably handsome man that she'd just been introduced to by a hyperactive seven-year-old.

By the time he stood in front of her, she felt ripped open and exposed. Those blue eyes, the ones he never took off her... could they see all her half-truths and the storms that raged inside of her?

She swallowed noticeably, her eyes darting around him and then to the ground. But then she remembered her transformation and all she's endured to get here. The redirected course she had put herself on, although she may not have known it at the time, had always been leading her into this moment.

She stuck her hand out toward him and pulled her shoulders back, determined to face the man in front of her. "Hi, I'm Callie. I'm a friend of..."

The look on his face silenced her.

Trey glanced at her outstretched hand briefly before connecting his eyes with hers once again. He grabbed her upper arm and headed into the barn, pulling her along with him a little more roughly than he intended.

Callie yelped in surprise as she struggled to keep up with him. Once inside, Trey released her roughly. "Who are you and what are you doing here?"

Callie stared at him, her mouth partly open, wondering what in the hell was wrong with him.

She folded her arms across her chest, shifting her weight onto one foot. He might be the most gorgeous man she'd ever seen, but she wasn't about to become one of those girls that lost it in the company of a handsome guy. And she certainly wasn't someone who would allow Mr. Handsome Guy to disrespect her for no reason.

"I'm sorry, can we try that again?" she bit out as she stuck her hand out toward him. "My name is Callie, and I'm your mother's friend. And just so you know, it's rude to go around touching strangers."

Trey searched her face, his eyes roaming back and forth between hers. What kind of game was this girl playing? He couldn't deny she was adorable standing there with her sassy attitude but did she really think he didn't know who she was? That happening upon a beautiful girl dancing in the middle of the road during a rainstorm was just a regular thing around here?

But then it struck him. She'd never seen his face. While she stood highlighted in the darkness by his headlights, he'd remained hidden in the dark inside of the truck.

She didn't know who he was.

A small smirk stretched across his lips as he realized his secret could remain his for a bit longer.

He stepped closer to her, gripping her small hand in his. And once again, her eyes glanced down to his chest and then back to his face. She smiled hesitantly at him. She didn't trust him. Smart girl. This game just got a whole lot more interesting.

"I'm so sorry, where are my manners? You said you were my mom's friend?"

"Yes, that's right. I'm here to help her." Callie's voice trailed off and Trey noticed the pink hue crawling up her neck.

"Are you a part of her gardening club?" He knew that his mom often had younger women come out to teach them tips on placement and irrigation tricks that helped his mom's flower beds become award-winning or at least they used to be.

"Yes. I just came up for a couple of days to run a few things by your Mom and see if I could help her with anything."

"Funny, my mom didn't mention inviting you." He loved that she was uncomfortable around him. It gave him an advantage that had often worked for him in past situations with beautiful blonde women.

"Really? Maybe it slipped her mind."

A silence stretched between them for several seconds before Trey realized he was still holding her hand. He shook it again, "I'm sorry," he rushed out, "I'm Trey O'Brien, Eve's youngest son." His voice faded out as he introduced himself as he had a million times before. Still, it was the first time since Jamie's death he had used that title – youngest son. He took back his hand, putting it into his pocket and looked at the ground.

The color drained from Trey's cheeks. "Are you feeling okay?" she asked. Her need to comfort him was overwhelming.

She reached up and lightly, tracing his cheek. Before, she would have never been as bold as to touch a stranger, but now things were different, she was different.

Trey twisted his face away from her, glaring while he moved away.

"Jesus," he whispered, as he reached up and brushed off the electric feel of her skin on his. "Didn't you just say it was rude to touch strangers?" He turned his back to her.

Callie's chest rose and fell rapidly. She placed her hand over her chest, hoping to calm herself from the sudden change in mood.

Trey pulled his cap off, squeezing it together in front of him as long strands of blonde hair fell onto his face. He felt hot and cold all at the same time as his emotions swirled around him.

"Listen...I don't think you should stay."

"Really? Why?"

He stared at the cap in his hands, shaking his head slowly. "Don't know. I just don't feel like it would be a good idea to have you around."

Callie watched as Trey's emotional conflict warred across his face. There were days when her storm won out too. Darkness was her blanket, the booming thunder of fear her comforting lullaby.

She cleared her throat, "You know what? I think I'll stay for a while. At least until your mom decides I've served my purpose."

Trey looked over his shoulder and Callie tipped her head to the side, smirking.

"Uncle Trey! I'm waiting!" Alex yelled.

"You'd better go," Callie nodded in Alex's direction.

He ran his hand through his hair, pushing the long strands back as he put his cap back on his head. Nodding, he replied, "Yeah, she's not exactly the patient type."

SIX

TREY WALKED A FEW FEET BEHIND CALLIE AND ALEX as they headed back toward the house. He watched as the two of them swung their locked hands back and forth between them, giggling about silly girl things. His heart skipped a beat when his Firefly flashed Callie a huge smile. He knew that smile. It was the one she used to give him. A heaviness settled somewhere inside of him. How could a smile, from one little girl have the power to affect him so deeply?

Alex looked over her shoulder and Trey gave her a quick wink. He struggled to pretend the very air he was breathing wasn't burning its way down his dry throat, but his smile felt so unnatural he gave up and looked toward the house instead.

Alex's sweet voice moved over Trey's skin like a pain he constantly craved, "Uncle Trey, would you come to my school? In a few weeks, I will be the Star of the Week. That means all week long I get to be first in line, I get to help the teacher, and me and my best friend, Elle, get to have lunch with the principal! Friday is my Star Day. That means all the people I love get to come to my class and meet all my friends."

Callie chanced a glance behind her, unsure if she should make eye contact with Trey after their odd exchange in the barn. She didn't trust herself around him, but she wasn't exactly sure why. Her heart picked up speed when she noticed his reddening face. His eyes were tired, maybe even a bit scared. She remembered this feeling, the bubbles that burst inside your chest as you decided what you want to commit to versus the actual reality of what you know you're capable of doing. Who would he lie to, Alex or himself?

She felt the need to say something for him, or maybe it was for Alex, but her words suddenly rushed out. "Your uncle Trey is pretty busy, sweetheart. I'm sure he needs to check with his work before he can give you an answer."

"No, no... I can make it." Trey's voice was breathy like he wasn't talking to people who were right in front of him.

"Really?"

"Um...sure, Firefly," Trey reassured.

"Yeah! And you, too, Callie. Will you come to my school?" Alex pulled on Callie's arm.

Callie dropped to one knee, looking at the beautiful, little girl in the eyes. "Well, I'm not sure I'll still be here."

Alex's shoulders dropped and she let out a small sigh. "Oh, you're going to be leaving?"

"Well, yes. Eventually. I'm only here to help your Grandma with a few things and then I will be on my way."

"Back to your house?" the little girl asked, too innocent to hide the disappointment in her voice.

Callie rubbed Alex's upper arms, comforting her.

"Well, no. Just moving on to the next place I need to be. But I'll make you a deal. If I'm still here helping your Grandma, I will be there for sure. If not, I will give your mom my phone number and she can send me the pictures from your Star Day. Deal?" Callie stood, smiling down at Alex.

"Deal!" Alex eagerly agreed and gave Callie a jumping high five, then ran past her toward the house. "Mama, Mama! Uncle Trey said he would come to my Star Day!"

Lauren walked out onto the porch followed by Andy, who stood a little too close to her for Trey's liking. Eve rose from the rocking chair she had been sitting in, a concerned look on her face.

Lauren's face hardened for a second before she recovered and softened again for her daughter's sake. "That's wonderful, sweetheart."

Alex ran past Lauren, "Yep. I'm sure he will be," she exclaimed as she raced inside saying something about cookies.

Callie stopped at the bottom of the steps and Lauren gave her a weak smile before addressing Trey who still stood a few feet behind her. He didn't know why, but he was sure it was a good idea to keep distance between himself and his rain dancer.

"Don't disappoint her, Trey."

"I won't, Sis. Just text me the time and I'll make sure I'm there."

"I'm not even sure I have your right number anymore. I've sent texts before and I never get a response, so I figured you changed your number."

"Same number, just not great at texting back." Trey moved his weight from one foot to the other, feeling the weight of his sister-in-law's disappointment.

Lauren just nodded her head as she looked at the shell of a person that used to be one of her best friends. She swallowed past the lump in her throat, trying to keep everything together.

It was bad enough to have lost Jamie, but they lost Trey at the same time. She would feel the absence of the O'Brien boys for the rest of her life but would be damned if she would let Trey do any more damage to her daughter just because she longed for his friendship.

"Okay," she whispered, letting her eyes fall to the ground. Andy reached out and lightly touched her elbow. She glanced back at him and smiled.

Trey pushed down the uncomfortable feeling rising in his chest as he glared at his best friend.

"Why did you need me to come here today?" He asked Eve as she came down the steps to meet him.

Eve's eyes darted to Callie.

"Well, Trey, do I need a reason to ask you to come to the farm?"

"No, it's just that you made it sound like it was an emergency."

"Heavens, no. I just wanted to see you and I also wanted you to meet Callie. She's going to be staying here for a little while."

Trey looked back and forth between his mom and Lauren.

"Okay? You had me stop in my dirty work clothes so you could introduce me to some girl you met in one of your online gardening groups?"

"Well, yes. I would also like you and Andy to clean out the guesthouse. She will be staying for a bit and I've been thinking about renting it out for some extra income anyway, so this is the perfect time to get it livable again."

A tingling sensation started at the base of his spine. He hadn't been out there since before Jamie had died. There was nothing good that would come from him spending time in that guesthouse.

"Mama, I'm sure Andy can clean that out without..."

"Damn it, Trey Grayson O'Brien! I ask very little of you these days, other than a few hours of your time here and there, and most of the time you act like even that is an incon- venience for you. If I ask you to clean out the guesthouse for my friend, you damn well better clean out the guesthouse. Do you understand me?"

"Yes, Ma'am," Trey answered without another thought.

"Good. You can start right now. Supper will be ready in one hour." She turned on her heels and headed back into the house yelling, "Girls!"

Lauren and Callie followed quickly without so much as a question, leaving Trey with the guy who used to be his best friend. That was until Andy had decided Jamie's widow was fair game.

Trey leveled his eyes onto him.

Andy stood motionless on the porch, his stare just as heavy on Trey. There were several minutes of silence before he spoke.

"How ya been, man?" he asked. The awkwardness between them thick with the time that had passed since they'd last seen each other.

Trey folded his arms across his chest. "Great. You need to mow the damn lawn and the barn needs to be painted."

Andy pinched his lips together and nodded his head slightly, pulling the dirty, old ballcap further down onto his head. He took a deep breath without responding. Andy had always been the type that thought things through, only spoke when he had something to say.

Heat burned up Trey's neck as he clenched his jaw. It had always irritated him that Andy seemed to have so much more control over his emotions than he did.

"Sorry. I'll make some calls about the barn. Today is mowing day so that'll be taken care of as soon as we get the guesthouse done."

Trey nodded once sharply. "Let's get this shit over. I have things I need to do." He turned back toward the guesthouse, his work boots crunching the gravel beneath him as he headed across the driveway.

"I'm sure you do," Andy mumbled under his breath as he climbed down the porch steps.

Trey swung open the screen door. The key he'd gotten from its hiding place underneath the fake rock out front trembled slightly in his hand. He pushed it into the lock on the old wooden door that led into the guesthouse. Trey felt Andy only a few feet behind him and the weight of having him there suddenly came crashing down around him. He paused and swallowed past the lump in his throat as his mom's words rang through his mind again. Trey took a deep breath and pushed the door open.

It was like walking into a time capsule. Eve had covered all the furniture with sheets, but other than that, everything was exactly the way Trey remembered. Something in his gut twisted and he fought against tears that threatened to fall.

The space was small, but to Trey, it was a mansion. His eyes moved over the open floor plan that he and his dad loved.

A memory of his parents playfully fighting flooded into his mind. "Jed O'Brien," Eve would scold, "if you love that guesthouse so much, then you can move your stuff out there.

Stop talking about taking walls out of my house! I love it just the way it is!"

"But Eve, a home is just a house if you aren't there," he would confess as he chased her around the kitchen.

He recalled the hours spent carving the railing that trailed up the open stairway, leading to the loft bedroom. To the right ran a wall of cabinets in an L shape that Trey and his dad had built by hand. He ran his hand over the top of the large island separating the kitchen and the living area. An original fireplace had been redone and covered in rock from the stream that ran along their property.

Trey's favorite part of the entire cabin was the floor-to-ceiling windows that lined the back wall looking out onto the sloped bank that led down to the stream. French doors opened to a porch that overlooked it all.

That's where Jamie had propsed to Lauren.

Trey stood frozen, not sure what to do first. Everything inside of him remembered this place. He wanted to feel comfortable – at ease. But instead, small drops of sweat formed on his brow as he tried to control his breathing.

This was the place he had spent countless hours with the two most important people in his life. It was never meant to be a place that crushed his spirit. It was supposed to be his safe place. A comfort that only home could bring. But now it just seems like a reminder of how far away he was from all those things.

"Are you okay?" Andy questioned as he laid a hand on Trey's shoulder.

Anger shot through him and he spun toward Andy, slamming a fist into his cheek. He watched as Andy stumbled backward, catching his balance just before falling to the floor.

"What the hell?"

Trey grabbed him by the front of the shirt, pushing him up against the wall and wrapped a hand around his neck, squeezing just enough to steal Andy's breath. He leaned in close, noses almost touching, yelling just inches from Andy's face. "Just what do you think you're doing with Lauren?"

Andy pushed against Trey's chest, "Damn it, Trey! Let me go," he sputtered out.

But Trey tightened his grip. "I will kill you before I let you touch her. Do you understand me? She belongs to Jamie and no one, not even you, will ever be good enough for her."

To Trey's surprise, Andy's fist caught him in the jaw, knocking him to the side as he stumbled and fell to the floor. Stars swirled in his head as he reached up to his jaw, moaning, and moving it around to make sure it wasn't broken.

Andy was leaned over with his hands on his knees, trying to catch his breath, and rubbing a hand down his neck, trying to regain his composure. He stood and walked over, looking down at Trey with a mix of anger, but also pity.

"You can be a real asshole, you know that?" He walked toward the door, not looking back. He reached down and grabbed his cap that had been knocked off when Trey first hit him. He placed it back onto his head as he walked out the door. "I won't tell your mom about this. It'll just break her heart. I'm going to tell her you wanted to do it on your own and I needed to get started on the mowing."

He stopped with one hand on the screen door and one on his hip. He ground his teeth together, shaking his head back and forth before taking a deep breath. "You've been gone a long time, brother."

Trey lifted his head, "Not long enough to be okay for

you to be screwing my sister-in-law." Trey laid back onto the floor, running his hand through his hair.

"You should come around more often. It makes your mom and the girls happy." The screen door slammed behind him and Trey was left alone with his memories.

SEVEN

CALLIE STOOD AT THE SCREEN DOOR, HER EYES FIXED on the guesthouse as she watched smoke billow up from the chimney. Trey hadn't come over for dinner.

They'd even sent the big gun, Alex, over to tell him it was time to eat. She'd come bouncing back inside announcing, "Uncle Trey said he's not in the mood to put up with this shit tonight."

"Alexandria!" Lauren gasped.

"I know, Mama. I was shocked too," she paused and pulled out a twenty-dollar bill from her pocket, waving it in the air like she had won the lottery, "but, he paid me well, so I told him we'd forgive him this time."

She ran out of the room, scolding over her shoulder, "But Gram, you really need to teach him to watch his cuss words when little kids are around."

Callie heard a shuffling behind her and turned as Lauren, Eve, and Andy entered the kitchen. She rested her back against the doorframe, inhaling deeply as a worried silence settled around them.

"I don't think he's coming in," Andy paused, looking past Callie and toward the guesthouse. "Maybe we should go to him."

"He just needs a little time. He's processing a lot right now," Eve said, leaning against the kitchen cupboards and wringing her hands in front of her. "He came here tonight. That's progress."

Lauren crossed the room, taking Eve's hands in hers. Her voice was gentle, but there was no way to soften the honesty in her words.

"Eve, it's been over two years. We're losing him. If we don't push, I'm scared he'll be gone forever. I can't stand the idea of losing them both, and I know you can't either."

Eve took in a ragged breath and closed her eyes, covering her mouth with one hand, her heart with the other.

Callie knew that look. She had seen it on her own mother's face many times when the doctors would tell them Callie's illness was stealing her life. It was the deep, emotional pain that manifested into physical pain when a mother was facing the idea of living without her own flesh and blood. She watched as Eve held tightly to herself, trying so desperately to keep it all together, but knowing to lose her youngest son would be the fatal rip to her already fragile heart.

Callie's heart suddenly felt heavy and she absentmindedly brushed her fingers over her chest.

"I'll go talk to him," she said quietly, surprising even herself.

"Oh, Callie. Do you think that's a good idea?" Eve asked, stepping toward her. "I'm just not sure."

Callie smiled weakly at Eve as she moved away from the door and joined her in the middle of the room. "I've seen this before in other grieving families. He's buried right now, lost in his grief and guilt. It's all he will allow himself to feel. He can't function without it and my guess is, he doesn't even know how to anymore."

"None of this is his fault," Eve said. She pointed a finger back and forth between her and Lauren. "We have never blamed him for any of it. How do we tell him that? How do we get that through to him?"

Callie pulled Eve into a hug before reaching for the aluminum foil covered plate sitting on the counter. She stilled, a tremor starting somewhere deep within her as she felt the importance of the moment.

"Don't take this wrong, but it's not about you guys. It's not about what you do or say, or how you get things across to him. It's all about him. He's doing this to himself. Deep down he knows you still love him, but sometimes that love isn't enough to make someone want to save themselves. He has to want to keep living."

"How do we find out what it is he needs?" Lauren questioned, looking back and forth between Andy and Callie. "We could help him."

"I'm not sure he even knows at this point," Callie said.

"Then how? How do we save him?"

Callie paused for a minute until finally raising both shoulders and shaking her head. "He saves himself. That's the only way."

Lauren turned into Andy and buried her face in his chest. He wrapped his arms around her and whispered into her ear. Eve placed a comforting hand on Lauren's back, tears streaming down her cheeks.

Callie, consumed in her own thoughts, turned toward the door as she continued, "He's afraid of what will happen if he allows himself to start living again. He's so convinced he deserves to be miserable that the idea of living free of his darkness terrifies him."

Callie left the kitchen, her last words hanging in the air. With a plate of food in hand, she headed toward the guest-house. Her heart pounded out a steady beat and she hoped with everything inside her that she was doing the right thing. There were so many ways this could go wrong.

Something had happened between Andy and Trey earlier, but Andy had dismissed it in front of the others. Callie wasn't exactly excited about being alone with a violent person, but she also knew Lauren was right, they were close to losing Trey completely. For Eve's sake, she had to try everything she could.

Callie stopped at the bottom of the steps that led to the side door of the guesthouse. She ran a hand lightly over her hair and grabbed the bottom of her braid. "This is silly," she said out loud to herself as she tried to swallow past a lump in her throat. She paced a few steps back and forth anyway. Trey didn't seem like the type of man who wanted to be coddled. He certainly wasn't in the right frame of mind for her to try to convince him that none of this was his fault.

She thought about Eve, Lauren, and little Alex. They all loved him so much and he couldn't see it...no, wouldn't let himself see it. He refused to see what he was doing to his family, and shame on him for shutting them out when they needed him the most. How dare he take advantage of his family's love like that? How thick-headed did he have to be not to realize how much they had sacrificed for him and the lengths they would go to make sure he was okay?

He was a foolish, selfish man who needed someone in his life to tell him exactly what he was doing to the people around him.

In the shadows of the setting sun, she made her plan.

She would start by marching right up those steps and telling Trey how rude it was to upset his mother by skipping the family dinner. He seemed like a guy who would want it all up front, no sugarcoating, just give him the truth. So that's what she was going to do. She would tell Mr. Hotty Pants O'Brien that his family needed him and he should wake up before it was too late.

Callie was fully engaged in her internal pep talk as she climbed the few stairs to the side door. And that's where she froze, looking in through the screen door and straight into the guesthouse.

It was breathtaking. Eve had shared with her the story of how the O'Brien boys, alongside their dad, had gutted and rebuilt the old work cabin, but she was entirely unprepared for the stunning craftsmanship that had obviously gone into each detail.

But even more beautiful than the hand-crafted stairs and the rich, stained planks on the walls, was Trey O'Brien.

He stood with his hands braced against the wood mantel, head hung low, staring into the fire. Callie's breath caught in her throat as she watched a million thoughts race over his beautiful face. The dancing flames highlighted his sandy blonde hair while keeping most of his face hidden in the shadows. Her eyes roamed across what she could see of his nearly perfect profile. His work shirt was gone, replaced by a clean, white t-shirt that stretched across his muscled back and clung tightly around his defined biceps.

A fierce wave of emotion suddenly hit her. Trey had lost so much too. The weight of Jamie's death was palpable within every aspect of Trey's life. In one moment, because of something he had no control over, his life had been hurled into a fiery abyss. And he'd surrendered to it.

Callie let out a small gasp, her shoulders dropping as

suddenly all of Trey's torn edges were apparent to her. His suffering was more than she could have ever imagined and she mimicked Eve's actions in the kitchen as she covered her own heart with her hand.

Shackled by her confusion, she found herself locked within a fierce internal battle. The need to protect him was so intense and she wanted nothing more than to be able to steal his pain away, even if that meant somehow carrying the burden herself. But her life was driven by a wild force of self-preservation now. One that recognized this was a dangerous situation and demanded a freefall away from him.

A small flutter began in her stomach as she reached for her braid once again. She glanced back at the house and then down to the plate in her hand. How could she have read this situation so badly? She was completely unprepared for this…and there was so much at stake.

"You coming in, or are you just going to stand there gawking?"

Callie startled at the sound of his husky voice, nearly dropping the plate. A shiver slid up her spine and she felt suspended in the moment. Not wanting to respond to him, fearful of how intensely she might feel his pain, she froze.

But her desire to understand the depth of his pain won out, so she steadied herself, took a deep breath, and stepped inside.

Trey didn't move. His eyes remained fixated on the fire as it continued to throw shadows across his face. Standing in front of her was just a man – ragged with destructive emotions warring against his own heart. It was both tragically beautiful and terrifying to watch as someone's soul tried to fade out.

She hurt for him, deeply. His sadness radiated around

the room and stole away all of her own securities she had built for protection. She felt heavy as tears threatened and she choked on her foolish struggle to say the right thing.

"What do you want, Callie?" His voice was neither angry nor inviting. It was void of any emotion, distant and detached. Not unlike how he lived the rest of his life.

"I'm sorry," Callie cringed when her voice came out just above a whisper. She wanted to appear less affected by him. Stronger. She cleared her throat and he turned his head to look at her. His intense stare made her feel something deep inside of her spark to life. "I didn't mean to bother you."

She opened the door and stepped inside. Callie shifted her weight as the silence stretched out between them. Trey kept his eyes on her, slowly perusing every dip and curve of her small frame. She felt stripped raw and vulnerable in his controlled stillness. She wasn't made for this. She thrived off movement and transformation. He was stagnant and unwilling to change. Still, there was something in the deep recesses of his eyes that held the spark she craved.

"I told Alex I wasn't hungry," he said roughly as he pushed himself away from the mantel.

He turned to face her, pushing both hands into the front pockets of his jeans, making them slip further down on his hips and exposing just a sliver of toned abs.

"We know what you told her and if you keep "telling her" things, she will have college paid for by the time she's in the fourth grade." The words rushed out of Callie's mouth as she turned away from him, trying to hide the flush that crept up her face.

The corner of Trey's mouth pulled into a smirk, but just as quickly it was gone.

"Your mom was worried about you not eating supper."

Callie took a few hesitant steps into the cabin and set the plate on the large island.

"Wow, this place is amazing," she whispered as she walked toward the staircase.

Trey followed her, watching as she ran her fingers across the hand-carved banister. "Your mom told me your dad gave you this place when you were just a boy." She looked at him and warmth coiled deep in her stomach as his green eyes connected with hers. She pointed up the stairwell.

Trey nodded his head, "Bedroom."

She dropped her eyes to the ground, clearing her throat. "She said you and your brother spent many hours out here working with your dad."

It wasn't a question, but when she looked back at him, he nodded his head again.

His eyes on her were like fire and ice and once again she was lost in him. An addicting mix of pain and comfort that she never knew she was hungry for until this very moment.

Needing to break the trance he had her under, she moved toward the windows overlooking the backyard.

"I can't imagine how important this place must be to you," she said reverently. She looked out to the stream as the sunset reflected in the water. "It's so beautiful."

His reflection in the window suddenly appeared behind her but he wasn't looking at the sunset. His eyes locked on her and she knew the battle that raged inside of him. His desire to survive and feel anything other than the emptiness was warring with the need to keep every emotion in check.

She held her breath as he reached out, lightly running his fingers down the thick braid that fell down the center of her back.

"Trey," she whispered, looking down, unsure what else to say.

He removed the elastic band and slowly began to unweave her hair. She shuddered as his hands moved higher, continuing to release her hair from the bonds. He took a step closer and leaned in, resting his head on hers. Slowly and ever so lightly, he ran his fingers up her arms and over her shoulders until he reached the nape of her neck. "I like it better down and wild," he said as one hand slid into her hair, parting and separating until it spread out against her back. He gently grabbed a handful and pulled her head back toward him as he wrapped an arm around her small waist. She gasped, shocked by the pleasure she felt, desperately reaching for his legs behind her.

The heat of his breath teased across her ear, making her knees weak. "What are you really doing here, Callie?"

She tried to speak, but Trey's touch had silenced her. His voice, his scent. She felt only him. His rapid breaths in her ear, his hand pressed against her stomach. He began a soft sway behind her. She closed her eyes, enjoying the gentle friction between their bodies.

He pulled her back even closer with a little more aggression and buried his face in her neck. She gasped, not because it hurt, but because it fed the fire in her veins.

"Answer me, Callie," he demanded. "Why are you here?"

"I'm here for your mom," she said breathlessly.

"Maybe..." he whispered as he teased the soft spot behind her ear with the tip of his tongue, tasting her, "you could be here for me, too?"

Callie once again caught their reflection in the window and it wasn't Trey she saw this time, but his brokenness.

What was she doing? She snapped out of her trance and

turned toward him. He was so close and all-consuming. Thick, corded arms reached out and wrapped around her waist pulling her closer. She placed her hands on his firm chest, hoping to keep some distance between them, but not really wanting it. Without looking up, because she knew she would be a goner if she looked into his eyes, she said, "I don't think that would be a good idea."

He buried his face in her hair, inhaling deeply, "I think it's a fantastic idea. No one needs to know. It could be our little secret," he paused, pulling her tightly against him. "Just like the dance we had last night."

Her eyes snapped up to his as she pushed against his chest and distanced herself. Oh my god, it was him. She felt heat creeping up her neck as she tried to control the twisting in her stomach.

He smirked down at her, lifting his arms out to the side as he spoke, "Now you can understand why I'm a little concerned about you being here."

She tried to walk around him, but he moved, blocking her path. "I'm worried that my mom suddenly meets some crazy, dancing in the rain, gardening girl on social media and invites her to our home to stay for a while."

"Yes, Trey. That's exactly what this is," her words rushed out as she pushed against his rock-hard chest again, trying to get him to move. "I'm the crazy one." He stepped to the side to let her go by, but she lost her balance. He reached for her, saving her from a fall, but used the opportunity to pull her tightly against his chest. Again. She shouldn't like it so much.

"Well, it seems like since you've shown up, my mom is barking orders at me, you're making promises to show up at my niece's school, and I'm getting in fist fights with my best friend."

Anger surged through Callie as she stood there, toe to toe, with this giant of a man.

"First off, let me go, you Neanderthal," she growled. Surprisingly, he released her. She righted herself before darting around him, just in case he got the notion to manhandle her again.

"And if I remember correctly, I wasn't the only crazy person dancing in the rain last night. You seemed to like it." She held two fingers up in the air and shook them in his direction, "Secondly, I didn't promise Alex anything. I clearly explained if I happened to be here still, I would come to her school and I will. You are the one who promised her, and in the short time I've been here, it seems like you have a real problem with breaking your word to the people you care about. And three..." she took the opportunity to poke a finger right into his chest as he closed the distance between them, "your mom yelled at you because you're an asshole! And that's probably the same reason your best friend punched you!"

He grabbed ahold of the finger she had poked him with and stared directly into her eyes. Her entire body shook with fear and anticipation, and something else she didn't want to acknowledge.

"I'm here because your mom asked me to come. That's the only reason and I will stay until she no longer needs me. If you think your assholery behavior is going to scare me off, please, I've faced much scarier things than Trey O'Brien."

She yanked her hand from his grip and marched past him. Needing to get out of there and as far away from Trey as she could, she headed for the door, but turned at the last second and grabbed the plate of food from the island.

His eyes widened, "Hey, that's for me!"

"I know," she said, smiling as she held the plate above the garbage can. "Have a great night. I'll see you around."

His eyes narrowed when he spoke, his voice low and promising. "You can count on it. I'll be keeping an eye on you."

"Looking forward to it," she snapped as she dropped the plate and stomped out the door.

EIGHT

"Morning, Sunshine!" Callie sang out as the water hit Trey in the face.

"What the," he roared as he sprang up from the floor in front of the fireplace. He ran his hand over his face, sputtering and pushing his wet hair back.

Callie strolled back to the kitchen, dropping the cup into the sink. "Your mom said you go to work early, so I thought I would help you out by making sure you get there on time."

His mouth hung open in disbelief as he watched her glide across the living room and throw back the heavy drapes that were pulled tight over the windows. He growled and covered his eyes as the sunlight flooded into the room.

She spun on her heels, tipping her head to the side and planting her hands firmly on her hips. Flashing him the most annoyingly cute smile he'd ever seen, she purred, "Aww, is Trey a grumpy grump in the morning?"

He shook his head, water flying in every direction. "Only when I get woken up by a crazy person."

She tipped her head back and let out a belly laugh,

"Well, you're in luck. This will be the only morning, ever, that I'm waking you up. Now get moving." She put her hands down, making a sweeping motion as she shooed him toward the door.

"And take this nasty stuff with you," she added as she kicked all the empty beer cans Trey had left on the floor around him last night, toward him. He paused for a second, watching her in shock. Who did this little blonde think she was?

She stopped for a second, opening her eyes wide like she was dealing with a child. Her arm suddenly came up and she pointed toward the door. "Well, get going," she ordered as she kicked a can in his direction.

He leaned down, stumbling as he tried to pick up the empty cans that rolled in his direction. His back was up against the screen door and he realized this was his final stand, "You seem to forget this is my guesthouse."

"Your mom says it's mine until I leave, so get your crap and get out."

"Whoa there, little girl. I did all of this with my own hands." He wildly pointed in a circle making sure she understood all of this was his work. "This is my land, my space, and my family. If I want to stay, I'm going to stay."

She quirked up an eyebrow at him, "Great. It's beautiful, they are wonderful and blah, blah, blah. Glad to hear it. Now get out."

"Blah, blah, blah?" he repeated, pushing his chest out and tipping his head to the side, questioning if she'd just said that.

"Yes...blah, blah, blah." She picked up his work boots and threw them at him as he stumbled back out the door. It slammed shut in front of him.

He had been effectively removed from the guesthouse by a 5'2, blonde honey badger.

"Did you seriously just blah, blah, blah all the work I've put into this place AND my entire family?" He stood there, watching her through the screen door as she brushed her hands together in front of her and smiled to herself like she had just taken out the trash. Suddenly her face lit up like she had an idea. She lifted a finger in the air and spun around, heading into the kitchen.

With her back to him, she called over her shoulder, "Of course not, your family is amazing. But you?"

A giddy, almost crazy laugh filled the cabin. Trey watched her until she opened the kitchen drawer he knew held the knives. Very sharp knives. He quickly grabbed his boots and all the empty cans he could, deciding it might be better to escape in case whatever crazy idea she just came up with involved him.

"Well, you really suck," she hollered.

He rushed to his truck and dumped everything into the bed. What the hell time was it anyway? It couldn't be much past sunrise. He looked at his watch...5:37 a.m. He shook his head as he ran a hand down his face.

Suddenly the door swung open and Trey startled, spinning around and facing her, holding his hands up in a defensive stance. Callie stepped out onto the small, wooden porch and laughed. "You sure look like a superhero there - barefoot and standing in your little boy undies," shaking the butcher knife at him. "The great Trey O'Brien huh? It looks to me like the mighty have fallen."

Trey looked down at himself, just now fully realizing he was only in his boxers. He didn't even have time to respond before she lined up the six, full beer cans he'd left in the refrigerator along the wooden railing and turned to go back inside. "Hmm...I wonder what else I can find in here?"

"No! No, crazy person! Do not touch my whiskey!" he shouted as he started toward the door.

Callie came bouncing back out onto the porch, whiskey bottle in hand, and laid the butcher knife next to the beer cans.

"What? This whiskey?" she asked in a questioning tone. "The whiskey you spent the evening with, even though your entire family was just across the yard?"

"Don't you dare judge me," he warned.

Callie lifted her shoulders to her ears and feigned innocence. "I don't know much about whiskey, but this stuff seems pretty expensive."

"Callie," his voice full of warning. "That bottle of whiskey is over one hundred dollars a bottle and I have to drive three counties over to get it!"

Her mouth fell open in mock surprise, "Really? Wow. It must be pretty good stuff."

She uncapped the lid and he froze as she tipped the bottle. He rushed toward her but not before she grabbed a full beer can and threw it at his head. He ducked, shocked at how hard this little woman could throw.

"Stop it, Callie," he said through gritted teeth. She looked him right in the eye and kept pouring.

She threw another beer, and another, draining the whiskey from the bottle between well-aimed throws.

"What's the matter, Trey?" she teased.

This time he rushed at her, she screamed and launched the empty bottle at him. He paused long enough for her to grab the knife, get inside, and slam the inside door, locking it before he could get in.

He grabbed the screen door, pounding on the inside door that he knew he would never be able to break down. "You're going to pay me back for that!"

He could hear her laughing inside as he backed away, staring at the door. He stomped bare-footed back toward his truck, picking up the empty bottle on the way. He mumbled a few obscenities to himself before turning back toward the cabin and yelling, "Blah, blah blah, huh? I'll show you blah, blah, blah!"

He slammed his truck door, his tires kicking up gravel and dirt as he sped out of the driveway.

Callie watched him leave through the kitchen window. She leaned against the sink, her head dropping down into her hands as she took in a slow deep breath. That was one of the hardest things she had ever done.

Don't you dare judge me. His voice echoed around in her head over and over. If he only knew that she was feeling the complete opposite.

She walked outside, standing on the side porch briefly before walking down the steps and picking up the beer cans, opening each one and pouring out the alcohol.

As she picked up the last can and held it away from her as she poured it out, she looked to the main house where Eve stood on the porch staring at her. Callie had hoped this would be over with and Trey would be gone before anyone else woke up.

Andy's truck pulled into the drive and past them both, parking in front of the barn. When Eve's eyes returned to her, Callie waved. Eve paused a worried look on her face but gave a small wave before she turned and went back into the house.

Callie's heart sank. She closed her eyes and whispered a

little prayer to anyone who would listen, "Please, don't let me screw this up."

She turned and walked back up the steps to the side door of the guesthouse. She wasn't sure what her next step was going to be, but she knew she had started something she would have to see to the end...whatever that end might be.

NINE

Trey sped down the gravel road toward his house. That woman was crazy...like diagnosable crazy.

Blah, blah, blah? What the hell? He didn't know what mental illness she had, but she had something! Or lots of somethings!

How dare she throw him not only out of the guesthouse but off his own land! He wasn't even sure what had just happened, only that he was sitting in his boxers in the cab of his truck driving a million miles an hour toward his house, and Callie was probably moving all her stuff into the guesthouse at this very moment.

And what did she mean his whiskey was more important than his family? Nothing was more important than them. She didn't know him, she didn't understand all the things his family had been through. She probably didn't even know the story. His mom wouldn't be naive enough to share the ins and outs of their family heartbreak with some stranger she met online, would she? No. She was too smart for that.

His mom's trusting face flashed in his mind and his grip

tightened on his steering wheel. What had she told Callie? Who did Callie think they were? What did she think of him? A prickling sensation started in his chest.

Callie had to go. His mom had made it clear she wanted Callie at the farm, but there was no way he could allow her to stay. She had a way of ripping open old wounds that had been long closed and he wasn't about ready to let a crazy person take over his family. But how was he going to make Callie leave without upsetting his mom even more?

He'd have to do this another way. Somehow make things so hard on Callie she would want to leave. But it needed to be her idea.

It dawned on him that he knew nothing about Callie, not even her last name. Panic swirled in his chest. He'd left her back on the farm with all the people he loved most in the world and he didn't even know her last name.

He turned into his driveway, parked his truck as close to the back door as possible and rushed to get inside.

"Where is it? What did I do with it?" Trey asked himself as he dumped the basket next to his computer and rummaged through the papers. He spun around, running into his bedroom and opening the drawer of the side table next to his bed. He ran his fingers through the pieces of paper he kept there, hoping the business card he was looking for would somehow be hidden in the sea of ignored mail.

He crossed his room, throwing on a clean pair of jeans and pulling a t-shirt over his head as he rushed into the bathroom to quickly brush his teeth. Opening the hall closet, he moved a few things around on the shelves. The pictures of Lauren and Alex caught his eye so he grabbed them. Shutting the closet door, he walked into the dining room and ran his hand through his hair. "Where the hell did I put that card?" he asked out loud to no one.

Then it came to him...he rushed into the kitchen, still clenching the photo frames in his hand.

The card was pinned to the board, right where his mom had hung it over two years ago. He plucked the card from its spot and shoved it into his pocket.

Realizing he was still holding the pictures, he headed back toward the closet but stopped as he passed the shelf he sat the images on before his mom's Sunday visits.

He looked down at the smiling faces before setting them on the shelf.

He picked up the phone and, without a second thought, dialed the number. He'd never called into work his entire life. Never taken a vacation, never been late, or left early.

"Hello, Mr. Gibbons, this is Trey O'Brien and I have... I have some family obligations I need to take care of. I need some time off. At least a week, but I will keep in contact with you if it looks like it might be longer."

After settling the details with his boss, he shoved his phone into his back pocket and headed back out the door. Sitting in his tailgate, he quickly pulled on his socks and boots he'd thrown in his truck bed when Callie had evicted him.

He left his own house as quickly as he had left the farm this morning, spewing gravel at the remnants of the water fountain that was surrounded by an Eve O'Brien, hand-made, wooden flower bed. It used to be a focal point when you drove onto his property, but now it was just a home for brown, dead weeds.

Heading back to his family farm, he reached for the card. Worth County Sheriff Jesse Deal had been a few years younger than his dad in school and the O'Brien's had always been some of Jesse's most prominent supporters.

"County Sheriff Deal," he answered and Trey smiled as he drove up the driveway of his family farm.

"Sheriff Deal, Trey O'Brien here."

"Hey, Trey. Good to hear from you. Is your mom okay?"

"Well, that's why I'm calling. I have a situation and I was wondering if you would help me out."

"Sure thing. What can I do for you?"

Trey pulled in front of the barn, sitting in his truck as he finished explaining to the Sheriff what he needed. He jumped out of the truck and a huge smile stretched across his face as he reached in the back for his tool belt.

Eve and Lauren stood on the porch, staring with surprise in their eyes.

"Good morning, ladies," he said with much more enthusiasm than he felt.

"Hey, son. What are you doing here?" his mom asked as he walked toward them.

Callie walked out onto the porch eyeing him suspiciously.

"Good morning again, crazy person."

She paused for just a second, exchanging confused looks with the other women on the porch.

"Asshole," she regarded him with a tip of her head like it was a respectable way to greet someone.

Eve swallowed nervously, looking back and forth between the two of them, clearly wanting to reprimand them both for their disrespect. She held her tongue.

"Trey, honey, don't you have to go to work?"

He shook his head, smiling at her. "Nope. I'm on vacation."

Eve's mouth fell open, "I'm sorry. What did you say?"

Andy walked around the side of the house just as Eve repeated what Trey had said, "Vacation?"

"Vacation," Trey repeated. "I noticed there are a few things around here that Andy could use help with. We've been slow at work so I called in today and told Mr. Gibbons I would be on vacation for as long as you guys needed me around here."

"Vacation," Eve said flatly, eyeing Trey.

Andy slapped Trey on the back, harder than necessary, almost breaking the fine line of control Trey had. Trey turned toward him, forcing a tight smile.

"Well, I think that's great," Andy said. "I sure could use some help fixing some of the fences around here. Oh, and I noticed some of the shutters on the back side of the house are a little loose since that last wind storm."

Trey reached for his work gloves that hung from his back pocket and slapped them against his hands. "Okay. Let's get started."

"I guess we'll see you boys at lunchtime then?" Eve asked, the questioning tone still present.

"Yes, Ma'am," Trey responded, smiling.

Eve turned and patted Callie on the arm as she passed by her. Callie gave her a warm smile as she watched her and Lauren go into the kitchen.

She crossed her arms in front of her chest and walked to the edge of the porch.

"I'll meet you out back," Andy said with a smirk as he put his cowboy hat back on and hurried off.

The smiles fell from both Callie and Trey's faces as they challenged each other with their silence.

Callie was the first to talk. "Vacation, huh?" she asked warily.

"Yep," he flashed her a bright-toothed smile that made her heart speed up.

"I guess I'll see you at lunch then?" she asked.

His voice dropped lower, the smile turning to a playful smirk. "Oh, you'll be seeing me all right. And I definitely... see you."

Fire raced through her veins as her body reacted to his words. In this moment, her wild side wanted to come out and play. She imagined running her fingers through his thick hair and wanted him to whisper into her ear like he had last night. She could feel the heat climbing up her neck – she knew she was blushing. She needed to get out of this situation and fast. She had gained the upper hand this morning but felt that quickly slipping away.

She nodded her head in his direction, saying her goodbye, "Asshole."

Trey tipped his hat at her, "Crazy girl."

Callie watched Trey walk away, fearing the rules had changed once again.

TEN

TREY CAME AROUND THE SIDE OF THE HOUSE CARRYING an armful of boards for the north fence. Sweat dripped down his face as he watched Callie kneel over one of the large planters running along the side of the house.

She wore her hair pulled up into a high ponytail, but it still reached the middle of her back. Her t-shirt sleeves were rolled up onto her shoulders, like girls do, to make sure she didn't get the classic farmer's tan lines. She wore short, grey athletic shorts that fit the curve of her ass like they were made for her. Trey couldn't help but stare and he let out a low whistle while walking toward her.

Callie looked over her shoulder, her eyes squinting against the sun. "Excuse me? What the hell are you staring at?"

Trey smiled. He liked her sassiness. "Well, you are most certainly crazy. We all know that. "

Callie stood, brushed the dirt from her knees, then crossed her arms in front of her chest. She tilted her head to the side, watching him closely as he closed the distance between them.

He wet his bottom lip with his tongue, biting it softly before he continued. "But even crazy can't stop a man from appreciating the fact you are all woman... and a gorgeous one."

He gave her a quick wink as he passed by her, dropping the boards into the bed of his truck.

"Trey, could you come here a minute?" Eve called out from the other side of the house.

Trey took off his work gloves as he walked over to where Callie had joined Eve on the ground, helping her lower a flowering bush into the freshly dug hole. He was glad to see his mom with her hands in the dirt. There was a sudden rush of memories from his childhood that made his heart hammer quickly in his chest.

"What's up?" he asked.

Eve started to stand and Trey rushed to offer her his hand. She laughed but accepted the help, brushing clumps of dirt off her gloves as she smiled at him.

"Thank you, Son. Do you think you could find time to run over to the nursery and pick up some more flowers for me? I would do it myself, but I need to get lunch started. And as you can see, I'm up to my elbows in dirt. It feels really good to be planting again, and to be honest..." she paused, looked down at Callie who was still adjusting the bush and moving soil around, and giggled, "I don't want to stop."

Trey was listening to his mom but couldn't take his eyes off Callie as she dug around in the fresh dirt. Maybe it was the fact he hadn't had a woman in his bed for a very long time, or maybe it was because there was no denying his attraction to Callie. Hell, call it a teenage wet dream, but it was damn hot watching that woman get dirty.

"Trey," Eve repeated his name, knowing she didn't have his full attention.

"Sorry. Yes, of course, I can."

Callie turned around, facing the two of them, but stayed seated on the ground, arms resting on her bent knees. She used the back of her glove to wipe away a few beads of sweat that threatened to run down her face, leaving a smear of dirt across her forehead. Trey put his hands on his hips and looked away smiling.

"Callie, can you think of anything we might need from the nursery?"

"Um..." Callie went through their inventory in her mind as she pulled off her gardening gloves. "Maybe some of the fertilizer we saw online this morning? Do you think they would carry it?"

Eve waved her hand in Trey's direction. "Oh, yes. It's the natural fertilizer in the blue bag. I can't remember the name though. Do you know which one I'm talking about?"

Trey shook his head, "Nope. I don't really search flower fertilizer online. You're going to have to give me more information than that."

Callie started to get up, "Let me go get my phone and I will send you..." she paused and looked up. Trey stood above her, extending a hand like he had to his mother. Her heart warmed as she hesitantly reached up and placed her hand in his.

His eyes darkened as their hands touched. Callie's stomach began to flutter and she knew she wasn't safe around this man. As much as she wanted to believe she knew what she was doing in this situation, Trey O'Brien was the epitome of a man in control.

He gently pulled her to her feet, standing closer to her than necessary. Without releasing her hand, he leaned into her slightly. The heat from both their bodies swirled together in a sweet ache of temptation and mistrust. Callie's breath hitched in her throat.

"Well, well, Miss Callie...I think this might be a ploy to get my phone number. All you needed to do was ask." Trey let his eyes leisurely explore hers until finally moving down to her lips.

Callie's face heated instantly. Her mouth fell open and when Trey's mouth turned up into a devilish smirk, she wasn't sure if she wanted to slap it or kiss it off his face.

"Why don't you get your phone and ride along with me?" He continued to hold her tightly against him, and although she pushed against him like she wanted to be released, that wasn't entirely true.

Eve was back on the ground and entirely engrossed in her planting. "That's a great idea."

Trey gently rubbed at the dirt smeared across Callie's forehead and she froze in his arms. He whispered, "Go get your phone and let's get going."

Callie didn't want to be told what to do. Part of her wanted to take a step back, look up at the arrogant man in front of her, and remind him he was a grown man who could surely find the right type of fertilizer on his own. However, there was another part of her that wanted to lean into the muscular chest, breathe in his manly scent, and do whatever he asked.

She found herself turning toward the house without question, trying to shake the fog from her head that had Trey's name written all over it. Suddenly, all the stories Lauren had told her of who Trey was before Jamie's death were becoming clearer. This man knew exactly how to get what he wanted from a woman. She smiled to herself as she thought maybe it wouldn't be so wrong to be another notch in his bedpost.

She grabbed her phone off the kitchen counter, pausing as she looked out the door. Callie watched as Trey stood next to his truck talking with Andy, who stood next to the barn. The conversation looked forced, not as comfortable as it should be between two lifelong best friends. The tension between the two was almost too painful to watch. Trey turned away from Andy, slamming the tailgate of the truck. Callie watched as Andy opened his mouth to say something but decided against it. He stood for only a minute as he looked at his friend's back, then disappeared into the barn.

A small tear escaped and she pulled in a deep, ragged breath. She pressed her hand lightly over her neck, comforted by the steady beat of her own pulse. Callie knew Trey truly believed he'd lost everything when Jamie died, but the truth was, he had made a choice to give it all up. He'd walked away from everyone. For a slight moment, she allowed herself to remember how close she'd come to making the same decision. How close she had been to giving up on everything and everyone.

She closed her eyes and whispered, "I will fix this. I promise."

STEPPING up onto the running board, she swung herself into the cab of Trey's work truck, puffing out her cheeks and releasing a big breath as she fastened her seatbelt. She saw the smirk on his face as he put the truck in reverse. He threw his arm over the back of the seats, checking behind him, and started backing out.

"Why do all of the guys around here have such big

trucks? It makes it a little hard for normal-sized people to get in." She folded her arms across her chest and lifted an eyebrow at him. "My best guess...you're all compensating."

Instead of putting the truck into drive, Trey shifted it into park, turned his body toward her, and smiled. He stretched his arm across the top of the seat behind her. The cab suddenly got very small and warm. Callie swallowed against a lump in her throat as her hands dropped to her lap. She looked away from his dominating stare. She felt like she might self-combust inside this God forsaken, super-sized truck.

"First of all, you aren't normal-sized." Trey lifted his hand from the back of the seat, running his fingers through a few strands of Callie's ponytail and watching as the soft hair slid out. His rough fingers found their way to her chin and he gently turned her face to look at him.

"And Callie, believe me... There is no need for compensating here."

He dropped his hand from her face, shifted the truck into drive and headed down the long driveway and onto the gravel road.

After a few miles of silence, Trey decided it was time to get some information.

"So, Crazy Person...where do you come from?"

She laughed sarcastically at his nickname for her. "Well, Asshole...what lifetime are you talking about?"

He glanced sideways at her, casting a confused look.

She inhaled deeply, "I may only be 23, but it feels like I've lived several lifetimes already."

"And that means?"

"I originally came from the east coast, but now I travel a lot. I guess my home is still the coast – at least that's where my family is – but I haven't been there for a while."

"So, you're homeless?"

"Oh, you would love that wouldn't you?" She made air quotes with her fingers like she was quoting a newspaper. "Homeless girl moves into guesthouse of unsuspecting farmer's widow."

Trey threw her another sideways glance, both of his eyebrows raised, a questioning look on his face.

She huffed, "No, Trey. I'm not homeless at all."

"But isn't the definition of homeless not having a place you come back to every night?"

"Why does that make someone homeless? And why does home have to be brick and mortar?"

Trey's face wrinkled as he shook his head like she was speaking a language he didn't understand. Lifting both hands from the steering wheel and raising his shoulders to his ears he said, "What the hell are you talking about now? Of course it needs to be structural – walls, a roof, a foundation. Those are all the things that make it a house. Without it, you don't have a home. Hence the meaning of homeless."

Callie threw her head back and laughed. "You really are self-absorbed, aren't you?"

Trey smiled. He liked the way her laugh made him feel. It was light and carefree, even if it came in the form of an insult to him.

"I'm waiting for your well thought out explanation," he teased.

A distant look suddenly crossed her face. It was like a mask had been removed and there was a pain underneath her cool cover he related to. Something haunted her and it seemed to be stealing everything from her. He knew she wasn't in the cab of his truck with him anymore, but somewhere deep in her head. He looked to the side of the road, fighting the desire to pull over, wrap his arms around her small frame and hold her against him tightly, protecting her from whatever memory was taking her away. His heart fluttered in his chest as his eyes darted back and forth between her and the road. He wanted her to come back to him.

He reached out and touched her hand. She flinched at his touch, looking first at where his skin connected with hers and then searching his eyes for something. Every cell inside of him fired off a warning, but he kept his face as calm as possible. "Lost you there for a second," he said softly as his thumb circled slowly on her bare leg.

Callie blinked rapidly, trying to clear the painful sting of her past life. "Yeah, sorry," she said, her eyebrows pulling together as she forced out a small chuckle. And just like that, the mask was back in place. Trey frowned and slowly removed his hand and gripped the wheel tightly. This girl was definitely hiding something.

"Back to what you said about being homeless. I think it's way more important to put your self-worth and security in something like your own heart, your own beliefs – your own kindness and your own thoughts. It's a safer bet than putting it in physical things. You say I'm homeless, but I can make my home wherever I am because I don't need the security of land and rooms and walls."

Trey drummed his fingers against the steering wheel, nodding his head and looking at the fields as they passed. His fields. His land. "You're a Gypsy then? You just wander from place to place?"

"I guess, but I don't really wander. I go with purpose and when I've filled that purpose, I move on. I don't expect you to understand because you are so heavily tied to your roots. I don't think there's anything wrong with that. You just can't understand the freedom of spirit I'm talking about."

"Why do you think that?"

"It's just something I feel about you." Callie made a sweeping motion in Trey's direction. "Everything is so controlled, so planned."

"There is nothing wrong with having things in line, Callie. It feels good to know things are going to happen the way you want them to."

"Nope, nothing wrong with it, except when things fall apart, then what? What do you do next?"

"Well, that's easy. You use the three R's."

"Huh?"

"It was my dad's saying. He used to preach it to Jamie and me all the time. When life isn't going the direction you want it to, you use the three R's. First, you regroup – that means going back to the beginning, reminding yourself what your goal was, and formulate a new plan. Next, you repair any of the damage done by your failed attempt. And the last R is regain. You regain your composure and move forward." Trey ran his hand over his mouth and glanced at Callie. "I haven't thought about that for a long time."

Callie bit the edge of her lip, thinking hard about what Trey had just told her. "The three R's, huh?"

"Yep. Jed O'Brien's words to live by." Trey looked across the cab at Callie, smiling as he remembered his dad. She returned his smile.

"I like it," she mused as she nodded her head and returned her eyes to the road.

And for some reason, her words made his heart skip a beat.

ELEVEN

THE RIDE BACK FROM THE NURSERY WAS QUIET...TOO quiet. And while it should've given Callie a reprieve from her constant reevaluation of the situation, it only made it worse. Why was he suddenly so relaxed? Why was he smiling? Why did he wave at everyone as they passed? Surely, he couldn't know all of them? And for the love of all things holy, why was he driving so damn slowly?

By the time they made it back to the farm, Callie was ready to crawl out of her skin. Parking between the side of the barn and the guesthouse, Trey jumped from the truck, smiled at her, and then disappeared.

She stayed in the truck, trying to figure out what the hell had just happened. This had to be another one of his games. The yelling, glaring smart-assy, Trey... That's the one she knew how to handle. This sweet, cordial, quiet Trey freaked her out.

Callie absentmindedly got out and walked to the rear of the truck, hoisting herself onto the bumper and then climbing into the bed.

"Whoa, what are you doing?" Trey asked as he walked back around the corner of the barn.

Callie jumped, his voice startling her. "I'm going to help you unload these bags of fertilizer."

"As much as the idea of you in the back of my truck, tossing around these bags makes me very happy in all the right ways," he waggled his eyebrows at her playfully, "it's not happening. Now come on out of there." Trey waved his hand, motioning her to come out of the truck.

Callie shifted her weight to one foot and crossed her arms over her chest. "Do you think I can't help you?"

"No...no, that's not what I'm trying to say. Come on now, just get down." He motioned again.

"Is this a girl thing? Do you honestly think I can't do this because I'm a woman?"

"What? No. You being female has nothing to do with it."

"What is it then? Am I not strong enough?"

"Callie, get out of the damn truck."

"No, I'm not getting out until you tell me why you think I am incapable of lifting these bags of fertilizer."

Trey dropped the tailgate of the truck and pointed to the ground.

"You have lost your ever-loving mind if you think I'm going to move with just a point of your finger. I'm not a dog."

Trey blew out an exasperated breath. "I don't think you're a dog. I just want you to get out of the truck so..."

Callie crouched down so she was eye to eye with him, poking a finger in his direction. "You can't tell me what to do. You can judge me all you want about how I live my life, how I dress, how short I am, but you cannot and will not order me around like a child."

"Then stop acting like one," he snapped.

At that very moment, Andy came around the corner of the barn in a skid loader. Callie looked toward the noise, giving Trey an opportunity he couldn't pass up. He grabbed her around the waist, intending on easily lowering her to the ground...except she was fighting his touch like it was causing electrical jolts to run through her body. "Relax, I've got you." He assured her as her feet touched the ground.

She turned on him, slapping at his ankles. "And I've got you, Trey! I've got you all figured out. You are just some man-child with a caveman complex who thinks women should fall at your feet because you look like a Greek God and then you flash your panty-dropping smile every time you want something."

Trey blew out an exasperated breath and moved toward her, crowding her with his body until she had no choice but to back up. For every step he took forward, she took one back until she was against the barn wall.

Callie glanced around Trey and watched as Andy lifted the pallet full of fertilizer bags, easily and quickly removing it from the back of the truck.

"I guess they loaded the fertilizer into the truck when I was looking at the rose bushes, huh?"

Trey nodded as he leaned into her, placing a hand on each side of her head caging her in. She held her breath and closed her eyes as he spoke right next to her ear. "I'm not sure what suddenly got you all riled up and I'm not going to say I don't like it, but let's be clear on one thing, okay?"

Callie nodded, unable to think with him this close.

"I didn't say you couldn't do it, Callie. To be honest, I'm pretty sure there isn't a thing you can't do. I just didn't want you to have to do it."

He pushed himself off the barn wall, taking a lazy

moment to let his eyes explore every curve of her body. "One day you're going to find someone who wants to take care of you in every way, Cal. And you're going to want him to...and it will be amazing."

He started toward the main house, pulling his work gloves from his back pocket before looking over his shoulder at her. "Let's see... man-child, caveman complex... and what was it, Greek God with a panty-dropping smile? I do believe, Crazy Girl, we have finally found something to agree on. You've got me all figured out."

CALLIE THREW OPEN the guesthouse door, marching inside the living room and pacing back and forth as she tried to calm herself. God, the man was infuriating and frustrating and beautiful and hot... and an asshole!

She needed to remember the last part.

It was so hard when he gave her glimpses of what she suspected was the man he used to be.

She was here for one reason and one only – to help Eve. And as soon as she could, she would get back in her little car and return to the freedom of the life she made for herself. She ran her hands over her face, growling to herself and wondering what she had gotten herself into. She wanted to run, wanted to grab the few items she had brought inside, and just move on. But she knew she could never do that to Eve. Not now, and not after everything this family had already been through.

She threw open the French doors and stepped out onto the deck. Her body hurt everywhere and the sunlight felt so good. She couldn't remember the last time she'd worked this hard before lunchtime. Eve had spent the morning teaching Callie the basic ins and outs of gardening and as much as she felt completely out of her element, she couldn't deny how much she enjoyed digging around in the dirt and listening to all the stories of Eve's life she openly shared.

She moved the patio furniture to the side and sat down on the warm boards, crossing her legs in front of her and rolling her head from side to side. She focused on her breathing and the constant comfort of her own heartbeat. Her body began to relax, releasing the tension she was holding on to. She focused on the warmth of the sunlight as it made its way through the tree limbs above, breathing in the mixture of smells only being this close to the water could bring.

She concentrated on the sound of her own breaths slowly filling her lungs and the controlled release of each that took all the tension with it. But no matter how hard she tried, her mind continued to go back to the green in Trey's eyes and the curve of his lips when he knew he had done something that affected her.

"Ughh!" She screamed out as she threw herself backward, closing her eyes and spreading out on the deck.

He wanted to know her name, wanted to know things about her. She rolled her head back and forth against the wooden deck. She wanted to know things about him, too. Wanted to see pictures of him as a boy, to know what position he played in baseball, who he took to his senior prom... What he thought made a man a man.

All things she had no business knowing.

And she wanted to tell him things. Share her experiences with him – her illness, the surgeries... What it was like to be a prisoner in your own body.

She wanted to tell him about the people she had helped

over the last two years. She knew he wasn't ready for any of it. He wasn't prepared for her.

But most of all, she wanted to tell him he wasn't alone. He didn't have to carry this burden. The life he was supposed to have, the one his mom and Lauren had hoped for him, was waiting for him. He just needed to choose it.

Happy, married with a family of his own – this could still be his. The small glimpses she'd gotten of his playful side warmed her heart. It filled her with the hope he could one day be that person again, but now she also understood how tragic it would be for this family if he never found his way back.

Trey was lost, not only to his family but to himself. The fear of coming back without Jamie was too high. He didn't know who he was supposed to be without his brother. She needed to figure out a way to reassure him that he wouldn't ever be the same person as he was before, and that was okay. He just needed to pick himself back up, even if it was piece by piece. The people who loved him were willing to wait. They're prepared for the pain and the fear and are eager to love him through it all. He needed to trust in that, everything else would fall into place.

Trey's voice echoed in Callie's mind, *I didn't say you couldn't do it, Callie. I just didn't want you to have to do it.* A warmth spread through her body as she rolled to her side so she could watch the rushing water of the nearby stream.

All she'd lived through and that man was going to be the death of her.

TWELVE

Trey pulled into the driveway of the farm at 5 AM, a smirk on his face as he parked in front of the barn instead of the guesthouse. He jumped from his truck, quietly closing the door, making sure not to wake anyone.

Today would be the day he began to break down the walls Callie had carefully constructed around herself. He'd seen her soften the few times he allowed himself to be kind to her. Soft words and helpful actions were the way he'd crumble her defenses. It should be easy for him since he'd been raised to treat a woman with respect, but this was under different circumstances.

When he was quiet in the truck yesterday, her frustration shot through the roof. He didn't really understand why being in comfortable silence with someone was what put Callie on edge, but he also didn't really care about the details of her personality quirks. What he did care about was how she felt in control within the chaos but struggled in the calm.

Grabbing the sack of food he'd brought from home, his mind flashed back to yesterday, recalling the fit she threw while standing in the back of his truck. Damn if she didn't look cute with her hands on her hips, holding her ground as she argued her point. It took everything inside him not to grab the woman and kiss the sass right off those perfect, pink lips.

She thought he was calling her weak because she was a woman. If she only knew the truth. The strongest people he'd known were women. Sure, being an O'Brien meant always being capable and playing the man role well, but he also knew his dad and Jamie pulled strength from their wives. His mom and Lauren were the ones who kept everything together.

Trey had meant what he said when he told her she could do anything she put her mind to. A woman who lived her life like Callie needed to be resourceful and capable. For the first time, he felt a twinge of jealousy toward her. The idea of being able to pick up and leave whenever the desire struck appealed to him on some level.

She had gotten defensive yesterday when he questioned the way she lived, and rightfully so. He didn't understand her lifestyle choice and as soon as he realized it was a sore spot for her, he started using it to try and get more information. He'd wanted to talk more about where she came from when they'd returned from the nursery.

That clearly didn't work.

But this...this would work. He had been perfecting this tactic since he was old enough to be interested in girls.

He looked toward the main house, pausing for just a second to appreciate how alive the place was starting to look. A rebirth had happened, not only with the lands but also within his Mom. And he knew it was all because of Callie. She was the breath of fresh air this family needed. But it didn't mean she could stay or that he wanted her to stay. Even for all the positive things she appeared to be doing, there was something about her that made him uneasy.

He kicked over a stone that sat next to the guesthouse, reaching down and snagging the extra key. He smiled to himself as he whispered, "Hello, hidden key Callie doesn't know about."

Once inside the guesthouse, he put the key into his pocket and placed the groceries on the island.

The sun had only begun to rise, peaking through the windows and gently lighting the center of the living room. He crept toward the stairs knowing Callie was up there because of her deep, rhythmic breaths that echoed from the loft bedroom and circled around him.

He paused for a moment, listening to the soft sound and pictured her upstairs, lost in her own wild dreamland. He hadn't slept soundly for so long, he'd almost forgotten the feeling of waking up rested. Every night for him was some new form of hell. Whether it be walking the hallways of his house, trying desperately to rid his mind of the flashbacks from the night Jamie died, or the miserable nightmares where he screamed for help as he clung to Jamie's lifeless body, waiting for someone to help.

He closed his eyes, absentmindedly matching the sounds of Callie's breaths with his own. He imagined her fast asleep, curled in the white sheets and down comforter he knew were covering the four-post, oak bed he'd made with his own hands. In his mind, her blonde hair fanned out around her with every inch of her creamy skin on display. He wanted to run his hands gently over her curves and watch as she arched toward his touch, her blue eyes silently begging him for more.

His eyes popped open when he heard her moving

around in the bed. A very unladylike groan, followed by a snort, more movement, and then silence once again.

He froze, not even wanting to breathe and not really knowing what he'd say if she suddenly appeared at the top of the open staircase. A surge of panic swirled in his chest. Had he crossed some line by letting himself in here? Was it creepy that he was standing here, listening to her breathe, and thinking about all the things he would do to her if she were his, all while she unknowingly slept upstairs in her false sense of security?

Her rhythmic breathing began again, and he let out the breath he was holding. No, this girl was not playing on fair ground and he needed to keep reminding himself of that. The usual rules didn't apply in this situation. She was the one who had shown up and brought with her more questions than answers.

It was his right to be here and he would catch her in her little game of lies and deceit or his name wasn't Trey O'Brien.

This entire plan had to start with chaos if it was going to work. Smart-ass comments and sass was where she was most comfortable. Those things made her feel like she had control. And that's when he would bring in the kindness – the stuff that made her uncomfortable – to catch her off guard with the hopes she would let something slip.

Maybe he would scream her name or slam two pots together yelling, "Wake up, sleepyhead!"

His dad used to do that tactic when he knew he and Jamie had been out all night and up to no good. He laughed remembering all the mornings his dad would wake him up because it was time to shovel shit.

The two brothers would spend the morning in the barn, doing as they were told, and throw up any remaining alcohol in their system. Jed would stop, lean on his pitchfork, and say, "This shit we're pitching looks better than the two of you. What kind of stories am I going to hear when I go into town?"

And they would spill everything. Where they were, what happened, and who they'd been with. Jed would listen, shaking his head as he continued to work. "One day, all of this is going to catch up with you boys and when it does, you better not look to me to get your sorry asses out of trouble. Do you understand?"

"Yes, sir," they would mumble.

"And you better hope your Mama doesn't hear about any of this. I swear you two will be the death of that poor woman."

Trey's stomach fell. He bet even his dad didn't know how accurate those words would prove to be. So many things had changed since those days.

But today was about getting information from Callie. She had opened up to him in the truck yesterday just enough for him to feel like maybe she trusted him. Even if that trust was small and conditional, it was something.

He dug around in the kitchen as quietly as possible, pulling out the pans he would need to make his famous, after sex breakfast. He began cracking the eggs and shredding the cheese.

This is a good plan, he thought to himself as he chopped the fresh vegetables then put the muffins in the oven. When he was ready, he would wake Callie up with a big surprise. Not the kind of surprise he enjoyed waking a woman up with – and he'd certainly love to wake Callie up that way – but this was a different situation and he needed a different outcome.

He watched as the coffee filtered down into the pot.

Once he woke her up, he would insist she come down for breakfast to eat. First, she would be confused at how he got in and upset he was there.

Then she would be angry because he thought he'd make everything better by making her breakfast. In her confused, semi-angry state, she would be throwing all kinds of insults and threats his way. This is when he'll bring in the big guns – a friendly smile here, a kind word there. Maybe even a bit of flirting if the situation allowed it. He might even throw in a wink.

Before she even realized what was happening, he would catch her off guard and slip in questions she wasn't ready for.

So, surprise her, feed her, and mix in some moves he'd perfected over the years that made women give him what he wanted. He was confident he would leave here with most of the information he needed to unearth the truth about Callie's intentions.

He smiled to himself, satisfied with his plan, and began pouring a cup of coffee. It was almost time for the Trey versus Callie games to start.

"Hey," Callie said softly from somewhere behind him.

Trey startled, turned toward her voice, and...holy shit. He knew right then and there this was a very bad plan.

Callie ambled toward the island, her long blonde hair wild and hanging loose around her face. Her sleepy eyes met with his and she gave him a small smile. Her cheeks were flushed a beautiful shade of pink from a good night's sleep. She slid her tongue over her lips as her eyes fell to the coffee cup in his hand.

She walked toward him...no, more like stalked toward him. A heat ignited in his chest at the sight of her and spread down to his stomach. He exhaled a trembling breath.

She wore fluffy, white pajama pants covered in pink lips and a tight, white t-shirt that read Kiss me like I'm dreaming.

And for a second, Trey thought maybe he was dreaming. He was sure the world had stopped turning, giving just the two of them this moment, and wondered what it would be like to have a woman like Callie belong to him.

She didn't stop until she was inches away from him, her fluffy sock-covered feet coming to rest between his. She wrapped both of her small hands around the coffee cup. Her fingers brushed softly against his as she took it and Trey used the opportunity to run his fingertips down each wrist to her elbows, then coming to rest on each hip. This wasn't exactly part of the plan but right now, she was too much to resist.

She closed her eyes, breathed in deeply, then glanced up at him through soft, brown lashes. "Smells like Heaven, doesn't it?"

Trey was breathless, paralyzed by her closeness.

She turned, shuffling away from him, setting the cup down long enough to climb onto the bar stool across from Trey. Pulling one leg up so it rested against the island, she reached for the cup again like it was her most prized possession.

Trey leaned back against the counter, bracing his hands on either side of him. He watched as she slowly raised the cup to her lips and took a drink. Did she just moan?

"So, you're having quite the love affair with the coffee," he said softly. "I might even be a little jealous."

It wasn't a lie.

Her eyes met his and Trey's heart was off and racing. Her voice was low and gravely as she spoke, more into the cup than directly at him. "Don't make this dirty. Coffee and I are in a committed relationship."

He chuckled as he turned, needing to snap the connection between them and wanting to get this rolling before he did something stupid...like kiss her. Damn, he really wanted to kiss her.

He grabbed a plate, piling on the hash browns. "I hope you like meat," he said as he slid the omelet onto Callie's plate, then rolled his eyes to himself. Jesus, did he seriously just ask her that?

He turned and Callie smirked.

"Ohhh, yes I do," she purred as she batted her eyelashes obnoxiously at him.

"Hilarious," he said flatly as he slid the plate over to her.

Her demeanor changed immediately when she saw the plate of food. "Oh my gosh, thank you! This looks delicious."

Trey grabbed another cup, filled it full of coffee, and watched as Callie shoved a big forkful of food into her mouth.

She moaned as she slowly chewed. Trey knew he was staring, but he couldn't help it.

"I was right, this is delicious."

Trey raised his cup to her in thanks, but before taking a drink, he asked, "Why weren't you surprised to see me here this morning? You should be pissed at me for invading your space."

Callie finished chewing before answering, wiping both sides of her mouth with her napkin. "It's the free spirit in me, I guess. I don't really have a space. I'm temporary."

He frowned. Didn't she understand how dangerous her lifestyle could be? What if he would've been some freak who wanted to hurt her? It bothered him that she'd used the word temporary to describe herself.

She continued, "I've been through a lot and I've learned to roll with whatever life throws at me. You know, like a random guy who stops to dance in the rain with me, and then a couple of days later surprises me with an amazing breakfast."

Their eyes connected and his heart fluttered in his chest. He wanted to believe everything coming out of her mouth was a lie or some sort of game. But this felt...honest.

Callie tipped her head to the side, a confused look crossing her beautiful face. "Why do you look sad? I said the breakfast was amazing and I think our dance in the rain was hot." She smiled at him over her fork, piercing him again with her untamed eyes.

A longing burned in his chest. A heaviness that both scared and excited him. He wanted to tame the wild inside of her. Not completely, not break her of it, but be master of its essence.

He wanted her feral spirit to respond to only him, his voice, his body. To have her shattering underneath him, screaming his name and giving all of herself over to him. This woman tempted him in ways he'd never known existed.

He cleared his throat, bringing himself back to the conversation. "First off, that sounds dangerous. You can't let just anyone have access to you. You need to take better care of yourself. And second, everyone needs to have their own space." And as an afterthought, he added under his breath, "And don't call yourself temporary. I don't like that." He took a quick drink from his cup.

She shrugged her shoulders and reached for her coffee mug, pushing it across the island toward him with a smirk.

"Ok boss, but it's like we talked about yesterday, I don't need that sort of thing. I'm happy. I'm free."

Trey turned back toward the coffee pot, Callie's empty cup in hand. "Well, while you're here, this can be your space. I promise I won't come in again uninvited. Maybe you'll decide you don't like being homeless and look for a place to grow your own roots."

She raised her eyebrows, bringing her shoulders to her ears and dropping them again, "Maybe, but I doubt it. Have I told you this is amazing?" she asked as she devoured another bite. "Where did you learn to cook like this?"

Trey handed her back a full cup and leaned against the island with both hands as he smiled at her. "My dad."

Callie raised her eyebrows at him, chewing another bite and waving her fork in the air, encouraging him to continue.

"He cooked breakfast for my mom every Sunday morning and as soon as we were old enough, he had my brother and I help. He always told us if we were ever lucky enough to find a woman who would love us, we needed to learn how to take care of her." He paused, smiling to himself. "He said a good woman will give you the world if you make her the center of yours."

"Sounds like your dad was a smart man," Callie said.

Trey smiled at her. "Yeah, he was one of the good guys."

"I bet you miss him terribly."

Trey's eyes fell to the floor. "I do. It comes in waves and at the strangest times. Sometimes it's in the middle of the night. Sometimes it's when I'm walking down the street. But yeah, I miss him a lot."

Callie continued to eat as she nodded her head. Trey laughed, "Are you getting full?"

"Actually, could I have a bit more of those hash browns? They are so good!"

"You can have whatever you want, Crazy Girl."

Callie flashed him a smile, a real one that lit up her face and warmed Trey's chest. She was a beautiful woman, even in her not-supposed-to-be-sexy, but sexy-as-hell pajamas.

He took her plate and spooned up another helping of hash browns and she took no time digging in when he handed back the plate.

"So," Callie drug the word out in a dramatic fashion, "what's the deal with you and Andy?"

Trey dropped his hands to his sides, clenching his fists tightly. This was not at all where he wanted the conversation to go, but he had to keep in control. His plan had already gone to shit, but it would be completely over if he let his anger about Andy seep in. "What do you mean?"

"Come on, you don't have to be a rocket scientist to see things are a bit tense between the two of you. And, if my memory serves me, you two were trading punches just a few days ago."

"It's complicated," he growled.

"Clearly." She paused, looking at him expectedly.

Trey grabbed a dishcloth and began wiping down the counter. His mind raced, thinking maybe if he opened up a little bit to her, she would feel more at ease and be willing to answer his questions. "I think he and Lauren might have a thing."

Callie dropped her fork onto her plate, the clanging sound bouncing off the walls. "Oh no," she feigned surprise, "what do you mean a thing? Like they're dating? They have feelings for each other?" She covered her mouth dramatically. "Are they sleeping together?"

Trey narrowed his eyes at Callie, "Yes. No. I don't know...all of the above." He began throwing dirty utensils into the sink.

Callie paused, feeling the mood in the room change. She softened her voice. "I'm sorry. I can see it bothers you. I shouldn't tease you about it."

Trey twisted the dishcloth in his hands. "It's okay. It's just..." He could barely hear anything over the sound of his own heartbeat pounding in his chest. "It's not appropriate." He turned away from her heavy stare, tossing the cloth into the sink. "He is supposed to be my best friend and she... well she's... "

"She's what?"

"She's Lauren."

"And you're mad because...?"

Trey braced himself with one hand against the kitchen counter, the other on his hip, staring at the floor. A volcano of emotions stirred inside of him. How was he supposed to explain this to her when he didn't understand it himself?

"Because you don't want her to be happy?" Callie asked.

"Of course, I want her to be happy."

Callie climbed from her seat and walked around the island. Her heart swelled in her chest at the sight of Trey's internal struggle, and even though she wanted to rush over and comfort him, she needed him to keep talking.

"Because you don't think she should move on? And she should just be alone?"

"No, of course not," he whispered, the sound of his breathlessness sending a chill across Callie's skin. "What would that do to Firefly if Lauren doesn't move on with her life?"

"So, you want her to move on, just not with someone else?"

Trey began pacing back and forth. "I don't know Callie," he said through gritted teeth.

"I mean, I think Andy is a great choice." She watched him pace a few more times before continuing. "He's kind, and handsome, and loves Alex already. He used to be your best friend, you have to know he's a great guy."

"He is, but it's not about Andy." Trey ran both hands through his hair before locking his fingers together behind his head. "I don't know, Callie. I'm not sure I know anything anymore."

"You want to know what I think?" Callie asked, closing the distance between them.

"No, but I have a feeling you're going to tell me anyway," he huffed as he crossed his arms over his chest.

Callie took a deep breath, trying to still the raging emotions that swirled in her mind. She lifted a shaking hand and placed it directly over his heart. "I think you're mad because it's proof the people you love are moving on without Jamie, and you don't know how to do that."

Anger flashed in his eyes as his expression hardened. He dropped his arms, pushing her hand from his chest. "Shut up," he seethed. "You have no idea what you're talking about." He rushed around her and stood in front of the unlit fireplace.

"Don't you think Lauren and Alex deserve to be loved?"

"Of course!" he yelled. Callie flinched but something inside of her told her to keep going.

Softly she said, "Someone who will make them breakfast on Sunday mornings, don't they deserve that?"

"Callie, stop it," he warned as he clenched his fists together at his sides.

"Don't they deserve to be the center of someone's world?"

With one swipe of his hand, Trey cleared the lamp from the stand next to the couch. "Yes! Yes, Callie. They deserve all of it and more! They deserve to be taken care of and pampered. They deserve to be safe and protected and feel like there is no one else in this world who is more important. They deserve love and laughter and the comfort of a family that would do anything for them. Yes! That's what they deserve!"

Making sure to keep the island between them, Callie pressed on but held her voice steady. "Then why are you so upset about them trying to find it?"

Trey resumed his pacing, his hands back in his hair, gripping and releasing it as tears filled his eyes. He was so lost, so alone in this moment, so defeated. His shoulders dropped as his eyes found hers and Callie was pulled into his hurricane. The look on his face pleaded with her to let it go, stop the pain he was feeling and allow him to continue in his darkness. "You don't understand," he whispered.

"Try me," she urged as she rounded the island toward him.

"You wouldn't understand."

She couldn't wait anymore. He needed someone, maybe even her. She refused to let him continue to go through this alone. "Explain it to me." She rushed to him and wrapped her arms around his waist, pressing her ear against his chest until she could hear his erratic heartbeat. "I'm here," she whispered.

He wrapped his strong arms around her, nearly breaking her with his attempt to hold on. He buried his face into her hair, shaking his head back and forth, "I can't...I can't do this."

"You can," she said, tightening her grip on him.

"They... " he began, his entire body shaking in her arms.

"Please, Trey. Let it out."

He relaxed his arms but didn't let her go. Running his

hands up her back and over her shoulders, he lifted her face towards him. One hand held her face, the other ran lightly over her cheek, tucking some hair behind her ear. A tear slid down his face as he rested his forehead against hers.

"They belong to Jamie," he whispered. "Only him. He's the one who was supposed to make them breakfast and tickle Firefly until she pees. He's supposed to be around to love Lauren like a goddamn champion. It's supposed to be him. If she moves on, they'll both forget it's supposed to be Jamie."

"Oh Trey," she sighed, as he pulled her close, sliding his cheek down hers, his tears mixing with her own. She whispered in his ear. "But Jamie is gone."

Trey stiffened in her arms and his eyes squeezed shut like she had just stolen all the air from his lungs. She watched the color drain from his face as he took a step away, dropping his hold on her.

When their eyes met again, there was a different Trey standing before her. Hardened and angry. The same Trey she had met in the barn her first day here. She messed up, she was losing him again.

"Don't you think I know that? And don't you think I know it's my fault that all the things they deserved, that the one person in their lives who was meant to make sure they had all those things is dead? I deal with that every day, Callie! Every. Single. Moment of my life is consumed with it."

Tears ran down her face. He was breaking and she was breaking right along with him. She wanted to tell him it wasn't his fault. He didn't kill his brother and he wasn't responsible for the decisions that lead to his death, but she knew this wasn't the time. But she also couldn't let this stop here.

"I understand Lauren belonged to Jamie. I don't think anyone who knew the two of them together would argue that. But Trey, doesn't she deserve to find love again?"

He stepped back into her, aggressive and terrifying, but she had to see this to the end. Her voice shook as she met him toe to toe. "What she had with your brother was something special. He was the love of her life. But he's gone and she deserves to feel like she's the center of someone's world again. And so do you."

That was the last straw. He grabbed her by the shoulders, pulling her to him, his face so close she could feel his hot breath. "Listen, I don't know why you're here or why you think this is your business. You are not part of my family and have absolutely no right to be talking to me about this."

He released her with a shove and she fell back, her foot catching on the leg of the misplaced side table. She slumped against the couch but caught herself before falling to the floor.

Trey reached into his pocket and slapped the spare key down on the counter on his way to the door. "Stay out of my way, Crazy Girl. I'm done with you."

THIRTEEN

CALLIE LAID WITH HER HEAD AGAINST THE BACK OF the overstuffed living room chair, staring at the exposed wooden beams that ran along the ceiling.

A week had passed with no word from Trey. He wasn't returning phone calls or answering the door when Eve went to his house. Thank God Andy had spoken with Mr. Gibbons who assured him that Trey was okay and at least showing up for work.

After sharing the story of what had happened between the two of them – minus the shove at the end that she only shared with Lauren and Andy – Eve had decided Trey needed space. So that's what they were all giving him.

Space.

Emptiness had settled in Callie's chest the moment Trey left and she had no idea how to deal with it. It made her jumpy and on edge. She was in a constant state of semi-panic. Had she caused irreparable damage? Pushed him too far? How could it be so easy for him to walk away from his family again?

The spot on her knee where she had hit the side table a

week ago was still swollen and bruised. She ran her hand over it and her stomach churned. She hated to lie to Eve but there was no way she could tell her the truth about what had happened. As far as Eve knew, she tripped carrying a flat of flowers, and that's all she would ever know.

Callie sat up, suddenly short of breath from the painful tightening of her chest. If Eve knew that Trey was responsible for the mark on her leg, Callie was sure she would say enough was enough and send her away. The thought made her stomach turn even more and she swallowed against the tightening in her throat.

She absentmindedly combed through her long, wet hair as she remembered the look in Trey's eyes when she'd said, "Jamie is gone." The pain that radiated through him hit her all over again. She groaned, threw her comb onto the chair, and covered her eyes with the palms of her hands. Why did she have to push him so hard? He apparently wasn't ready for that. And now he was gone, away from his home, away from his family and away from her.

Callie stood, moving slowly when her muscles complained. She was sore and tired from planting flowers into decorative planters that would sit along the barn. Eve had agreed to host a BBQ for family and friends to kick off Daisy Days – a town celebration that happened every year.

She'd hosted the event up until Jamie's death. This would be the first time in over two years she had invited people back to the farm. Although everyone was very excited to see Eve doing what she loved, with her attention shifting to the planning aspect of feeding so many people, it left all the planting and yard work to Callie and Andy.

She'd used an online gardening group to cover up the truth of how she'd met Eve. In reality, she'd never planted anything until stepping onto the O'Brien's land. Eve was a fantastic teacher and Callie had come to find that not only did she really enjoy having her hands in the dirt, but she was also good at it.

A knock at the door startled her and she turned to see Eve standing there smiling. She rushed to the door, "Eve, please. You don't have to knock. This is your home."

"Well yes, sweetheart, but this is your space." Callie's heart seized as Eve echoed the same words Trey had said to her the last time he was here.

"Lauren, Alex, and Andy are going to the movies tonight so I guess it's just you and me. I need to go to the grocery store. They have the farmer's market tonight and I would like you to come with me," Eve insisted. "And then maybe we could stop at the pizza place in town and grab something to eat."

"That sounds fabulous, let me get my shoes," Callie said as she went toward the door and slipped into her flats.

Eve moved further into the living room, finally stopping at the windows overlooking the stream.

The mood in the room suddenly changed, leaving Callie unsure what to do. She waited in the heavy silence, giving Eve as much time as she needed and hoping her presence was enough. She wasn't sure she could talk about Trey right now without all her secrets becoming painfully obvious.

A small shudder took over Eve's body and she ran her hands up and down her arms as she continued to stare out the window. "This wasn't how my life was supposed to go." Eve reached out and touched the glass in front of her as if touching a long-lost memory.

"I was supposed to grow old with Jed, watch my sons raise a bunch of grandbabies, and..." Eve's voice broke as her words faded out. "What happened to my family, Callie?"

"He'll come back,' Callie said with much more confidence than she felt.

"But at what cost? He's miserable when he's here. Everything reminds him of Jed and Jamie. He carries so much guilt and shame, I don't know how to help him."

"I think he just needs time. He needs to be reminded of what's actually important and what he's giving up."

Eve pulled her hand away from the window, lowering her eyes to the ground. "Maybe I need to just let him go."

"What? No. You don't mean that," Callie said gently, turning Eve to face her.

"I lay awake at night trying to figure out what Jed would do if he were still alive. How would he handle this? He had such a special relationship with the boys. They trusted him, told him things they didn't tell me. How would he break through Trey's thick head to make him realize what he was doing to all of us?"

"He'd probably have them both out in the barn shoveling shit," Callie uttered.

Eve tried to laugh, but it was a sad sound, "You're probably right."

Callie gave Eve's shoulders a gentle squeeze. "I don't know the answer to any of your questions, but I do know Trey loves you so much. He's still the same boy that you raised. He has a huge heart and that's probably why he's feeling this so deeply."

Eve nodded her head in agreement but Callie could see the uncertainty in her eyes.

"You know," Eve said, "it takes a special kind of woman to love an O'Brien."

Callie dropped her hands from Eve's shoulders, surprised by the change in conversation. "I think you're all pretty easy to love, actually."

"I'm talking about real love. Oh, believe me, I've seen lots of lust and obsession. Trey has never had trouble getting the attention of girls – it was almost a gift." Eve paused, a small smile gracing her lips. She waved a hand in the air as she continued. "He just flashes that smile and turns on the charm and girls flock to him."

"I can certainly see where that would be true."

"But it takes someone exceptional to see beyond all of that. Beyond the charm, beyond the handsome face. Behind all of that, you'll find the stubbornness, the one-track mind, and the bull-headedness that he has... that they all had. I know you've seen the ugly side of Trey, the side that most don't see. I want to apologize for that, he can be a real asshole sometimes."

"You don't know the half of it," Callie mumbled.

"But you're still here, and don't flatter me by saying it's all for me, sweet girl."

Callie's heart began to pound in her chest as a swarm of butterflies let loose in her stomach. "We should get going." She turned toward the door as she felt warmth crawling up her face. The walls seemed to be closing in on her.

"You know what's harder than missing an O'Brien boy, Callie?"

Callie paused, shaking her head and looking over her shoulder at Eve.

"Loving one."

Callie exhaled a long breath and Eve reached for her hands. "I love my son. He is precious to me. And I may act like I don't see the interactions between the two of you, but I do. And under different circumstances or at a different time, maybe, but..."

Callie's eyes flooded with tears and she tried to swallow

past the burn at the back of her throat. She watched help-lessly as Eve struggled to find her words.

"Callie, please protect yourself. Don't fall in love with him. He will hurt you. He's never been the commitment type and this," she pointed between the two of them, "has already become so much more than what I intended it to be. I didn't know you would come here and it would feel so natural between all of us. I don't want you to get hurt. I don't want him to get hurt. And if something happens between the two of you, I don't see it ending well."

"Eve, I don't –" tears began to fall as she tried to speak lies that had already been stolen by the truth in her heart.

"Sweetheart, I see it in your eyes. You crave his pres-ence just as deeply as I feel his absence. Jed and I used to joke about feeling each other. It sounds so silly now, but I would try to sneak into the barn when I knew he was busy with something, and every time, without fail, he would say, I feel you, my love."

Callie looked away as she wiped at her falling tears, trying to calm the racing thoughts she had swarming in her head. She cared about Trey, but had she let it go as far as love? Had she gotten so lost in Trey's world that every wall she'd so perfectly constructed over the years fell without warning?

"I may be too late, maybe your feelings already run too deep and you just haven't admitted it to yourself yet. Just promise me you'll try. I love having you here and you are welcome to stay, but please don't blur the lines of what we are trying to accomplish. It could be dangerous for all of us."

Callie forced a smile, nodding as Eve pulled her in for a tight hug.

Oltman's grocery store was on the corner of Main Street. It was the only grocery store in town and apparently the place to be on a Wednesday evening. Large speakers sitting outside the back doors of the store played a constant loop of the latest country hits. Callie let a small squeal escape as Jason Aldean started playing. God, she loved that man.

Half of the parking lot was filled with colorful booths filled with vendors peddling fresh vegetables and fruits and anything else you could possibly want. Callie noticed one table had an exceptionally long line.

"What's the big attraction over there?" Callie inquired.

Eve leaned into Callie, talking just above a whisper. "Well, the two ladies at that table are authors."

"Really?" Callie asked with a smile as she watched Eve's eyes light up.

"That's right. They live two towns over."

"I love reading. What genre do they write?"

Eve patted Callie's arm at the same time she waved to some of the other ladies standing in line. "I believe they call it mommy porn, dear."

Callie nodded and gave Eve a broad smile. "Whatever floats your boat, I guess."

"I love that stuff," Eve said giggling. "Those are the ladies from my book club. They're the best! I'll be right back." She scooted off toward the other women who waited in line.

Callie weaved in and out of the crowd, browsing through the tables of candles and homemade wooden signs. The vibe was happy and upbeat and she loved it.

She found herself in front of a brightly colored stand, talking with a nice man and his wife about how to pick out the right tomato.

"I didn't know you liked tomatoes," his calm voice slid over her skin, igniting goosebumps everywhere. She froze, carefully setting the tomato back onto the table and pushing her tongue over her suddenly dry lips.

Unable to turn around and face him, she stated, "I don't. I was buying them to throw at you the next time you tried to sneak into the guesthouse."

A low throaty laugh calmed her nerves a bit until Trey leaned in closer to her ear. A shockwave crashed through her entire body as she felt his warmth. "Hello, Callie," he whispered. And that's when she noticed the smell of alcohol on his breath.

She turned and her voice cracked as she tried to speak. "Trey."

He was unshaven and his clothes looked like he'd been wearing them for days. Her eyebrows pulled together as she looked him over from head to toe. Even in this state, and as worry flooded through her, she still thought he was the most handsome man she'd ever seen.

"I see you've missed me," he said with a smirk.

Callie shifted her weight from one side to the other and pushed her hands into her front pockets. She averted her eyes, not able to look directly at him. "No. I personally think it's been a nice reprieve. Your mother, however, has missed you terribly. Shame on you for dropping off the face of the earth like that." She snuck a quick look in his direction.

Trey pressed his lips together, looking over Callie's head. "I would think my mother would be used to it by now." Trey paused, then pointed a finger at her, "And you're lying. I can see how much you missed me. You have a terrible poker face."

He turned and headed into the store, Callie hurried behind him. "Well, you're drunk and... don't walk away from me when I'm still talking to you."

"Oh, I'm sorry. Were you still talking?" Trey kept

walking while Callie tried to keep up with him. "There's actually a difference between talking and just flapping your lips when you don't know what the hell you're saying." He stopped abruptly and turned around, Callie nearly plowed into him. "And I'm not drunk..." he smiled down at her, "but I'm working on it." He added a wink for good measure as he turned back around and sauntered away from her.

"You are such an asshole. Wait up!"

"Why would I wait for you when you just called me an asshole?"

"Okay, I'm sorry. Just hold up a second and let me talk to you."

"No Callie, I don't think I'll do that."

He turned down the aisle where the chips were and picked up speed.

"Just wait for a second, Trey. If you don't want to talk to me fine, at least go find your mom." She lunged forward, grabbing his arm.

"What do you want from me?" he growled as he spun around, yanking his arm out of her grip.

She put her hands up in front of her, "Listen, I'm sorry if I spoke out of line the last time we were together."

Trey huffed out a breath and rolled his eyes as he crossed his arms over his chest.

"You have two minutes to speak. Go."

"Um, I guess I just wanted you to know that I never meant to hurt you."

"Time's up." He turned and continued down the aisle and away from Callie. She struggled between walking and running to keep up with his long legs as he turned the corner, headed for the back of the store.

"Trey, wait. That was nowhere near two minutes. Please."

He stopped in front of the coolers, browsing as Callie continued to talk, reaching in and grabbing a twelve pack of his favorite beer.

"I shouldn't have pushed you that hard. It's none of my business."

"That's right, it's not. But here you are, standing in front of me again talking about shit you know nothing about. Who are you? Why are you here? What do you want?"

Callie froze at his questions. Her earlier conversation with Eve echoed in her head. *This has gone farther than I ever wanted it to.*

Callie opened her mouth to speak but nothing came out. The truth was so close, all she needed to do was say the words. Tell him why she was here. It would feel so good to let it all out. But once again, she thought of Eve. Even though she had said it might be better to let him go, she knew Eve didn't mean it, and Callie knew she held the truth that could finally break Trey. The truth couldn't be told here with no family around to support him.

She watched as Trey's face reddened. He leaned down so they were face to face. "Can't come up with a believable lie quick enough?"

He started toward the front of the store and Callie followed him to the checkout line. "Listen...this is a conversation you need to be having with your family, not me."

"Well how convenient. Now you want to tell me the truth, but not without my family, and I bet that talk can only happen at the farm, right?"

The checkout girl scanned his items and announced his total. He threw his money at her, "Keep the change, Tara. Sorry for the crazy person." He made a circle motion at his temple and then pointed back at Callie. The checkout girl stood stiff and her eyes went wide. Her mouth opened slightly to respond but then snapped closed again and looked in Callie's direction. Trey took off toward the exit and Callie said to the girl, "I'm so sorry. I'm really not crazy."

"Yes she is!" Trey hollered over his shoulder as he walked out the door. Callie squeezed her eyes shut and pinched the bridge of her nose.

A few seconds of silence ticked by until Tara finally spoke. "Um, Callie, is it?"

Callie opened her eyes and Tara pointed toward the parking lot. "You'd better go if you're going to catch him."

Callie gasped as she rushed after him.

"Let me guess, you're going to manipulate me into coming back to the farm so you can point out to me that not only am I a total asshole, but I also want my entire family to be unhappy for the rest of their lives?" he gruffly asked as she approached him.

"What? No..." she panted as she tried to catch her breath.

"Well isn't that basically what you told me in our last conversation?" He pulled down the tailgate of his truck, setting his beer inside.

Her mind raced through the conversation they had had at the guesthouse. Is that really what she had done? Had she placed blame? Made him feel even worse than he already did?

She closed her eyes and covered her mouth with one hand. How could she be screwing this up so badly? She had to fix it but didn't know how.

She reached for him, lightly touching his t-shirt. "I'm so sorry I made you feel that way."

With lightning fast speed, he spun around, grabbing her around the waist and lifted her onto the tailgate. She gasped as he stepped between her legs, pulling her tightly against him.

He leaned in, his wild eyes searching her face, ending on her lips. Her heart beat at a frantic pace, pumping desire through her veins and stealing away anything that wasn't the man in front of her.

Trey didn't know where they would go from here – from this moment where the rest of the world was invisible and all that remained was the beauty before him – but he needed this. Just below the surface, he raged like a burning fire and she was the calming winds his soul needed. His head spun, intoxicated by the feel of her body pressed against his.

What was he thinking? He couldn't do this... he shouldn't. He had nothing to offer her, he was broken beyond repair. She was free and beautiful and secure and his heartache would only anchor her to him.

"Don't ever be sorry about who you are, Callie."

She was breathless and he loved how he affected her. He wanted to tell her what she did to him, too. Somehow, even though the words she spoke to him were painful, he knew they were all true. He also knew no one in the world would've been able to express such truths to him in the way she did. He should walk away right now, spare her of all the garbage that would come crashing down around her if she started having feelings for him.

With one hand on the side of her face, his other gripping her hip and holding her in place, he leaned in closer, searching her eyes with a fierce recklessness that stripped everything away. "You were right about one thing, Callie," he whispered. "I am an asshole."

His lips crashed against hers. It was aggressive and possessive. She matched every lick, and suck, and nibble with him, trading dominance and submission back and forth.

He ran his tongue across her bottom lip and she opened for him, moaning as he ran his fingers into her hair. It was wild and free, like her, but controlled at the same time, like Trey.

He broke away and she whimpered, trying to keep him close. He pressed his forehead to hers.

He couldn't do this. He felt her too profoundly and every part of him wanted to give in to her. She'd seeped into his mind with every minute that passed by. There was no way he could let her into his darkness. It would strip her of all the freedoms she held so dear. His heart was in pieces, broken beyond repair, and barely beating. But that was his prison cell, he wouldn't let it become hers.

"I knew it," he whispered.

Lifting her off his truck, he put her feet on the ground, but she refused to let him go. She twisted her fists into his t-shirt, afraid of what would happen if she released him. He ran his hands down both sides of her hair. He loved it when she let it hang down in waves.

"What? What did you know?" she asked. Her voice was soft and breathless.

"I knew kissing you would feel like that." He tucked a strand of hair behind her ear before touching his lips to her forehead.

He needed to leave...now. He was so close to picking her up, putting her in his truck, and driving. Driving until they ran out of gas, driving until she asked him to stop, driving until there was nothing but him and Callie.

But that was not reality for him. He knew his demons would follow, so he let her go.

"Just wait. Hold on...please." He could hear the desperation in her voice and it was almost his undoing.

She followed him around the side of the truck. He got in and shut the door, looking at her through the open truck window. Her eyes glistened with unshed tears as she grabbed at the door handle.

"Hold on," she begged.

He gripped the steering wheel hard, trying desperately to keep control. "Hold on? Hold on to what, Callie?"

Callie slid her hand around the back of Trey's neck. He leaned into her touch, closing his eyes for a second before pulling her hand away and placing a soft kiss on her palm.

"To me," she whispered. "Just hold onto me."

He put the truck into drive.

Her eyes darted to the gear shift and then frantically back to him. "Wait, don't leave! Not again."

Trey's eyes softened, "It's all I know how to do anymore," he said, "and it's better for everyone."

She took a timid step back, watching as he pulled out of the parking lot.

Tears rolled down her cheeks. She crossed her arms around her midsection, trying to fight off the terrible ache in her stomach. She was lost again, unsure what to do next. Her ragged breaths painfully filled her lungs when all she really wanted to do was scream out.

And across the parking lot stood Eve and her friends, watching it all. Everyone watched.

She stood frozen in the spot where Trey's truck had been as Eve cut through the crowd walking toward her. As soon as she could, Eve pulled her into a tight embrace, protecting her from the prying eyes of the town. "I tried, I really did. I'm sorry, but you were right. Your talk," she sobbed into Eve's shoulder, "I guess it came a little too late."

Eve took a deep breath, exhaling quickly and pushing Callie back to look into her eyes. "Love is love. It's demanding, agonizing, and at times can be a downright bitch. But it's the one thing we all crave. When it's right, it's incredible and there's nothing else like it."

Callie nodded her head and wiped the tears from her cheeks.

"Don't worry," Eve said. "What's done is done. We'll figure this all out. But first, let's go eat pizza."

FOURTEEN

Trey rubbed his hand down his face, mumbling to himself as he shuffled through his dark dining room toward the back door. Who would be knocking at nearly midnight?

He'd barely gotten the door open before a fist came flying and connected with his jaw. White lights exploded behind his eyelids. He stumbled backward after another blow landed on the side of his head. He spun, trying to catch himself on the kitchen counter and stay upright before his assailant could get in another punch.

"You piece of shit!" Andy barked as he flipped on the light and charged into the house after him. "I can't believe your Daddy hasn't risen from his grave to beat the shit out of you himself."

"What's gotten into you?" Trey shouted as he shielded his face with his arms. Andy grabbed his shirt with both hands and backed him up through the kitchen and into the living room.

"If it weren't for those girls back at the farm who are so damned worried about you, I would give you the worst ass kicking of your life right now." Andy tightened his fists in

Trey's shirt and pulled him in even closer. "You're an embarrassment to all of us."

Trey shoved him off. "What the hell? You've lost your damn mind if you think you're going to come into my house —"

Andy stepped closer and pointed a finger inches from Trey's face roaring at him, "Did you push Callie?" He grabbed Trey again. "Don't even try to lie to me! I know you pushed her last week when you surprised her with breakfast." Andy shoved Trey and he fell against the couch, his back against the cushions. "Let's not even talk about how out of line it was for you to let yourself in while she was sleeping!"

Trey ran his hands through his hair as Andy paced in front of him. "I know...I just needed some answers. It was stupid and she's making me crazy," Trey groaned.

"Stupid? You think it was stupid? It was so beyond stupid! Your brother would beat you until you couldn't walk if he were here! You have no idea the kind of damage you could've done by shoving her like that!"

Trey covered his face with his hands. He knew he'd lost control and shoved Callie out of his way. The moment had replayed a million times over in his mind and it was the guilt that was keeping him away.

"And you want to know something funny? After she told me what happened, she begged me not to come here. She cried, you piece of shit. She said she was sure you didn't mean to hurt her and you were just angry at the situation. She fucking protected you. Can you believe that?"

"Oh my God," Trey sighed, looking away from him. "Did I hurt her?"

Trey's stomach sank as Andy's face became even redder and he clenched his fists open and shut.

"Well I don't know, Trey," he snarled, his voice shaking. "What do you think? She's tiny, and you shoved her into a table. Of course you hurt her! She has a huge bruise on her leg."

Trey covered his eyes with the palms of his hands and groaned as he slid further down onto the couch. He couldn't handle hearing he had hurt her. What the hell was wrong with him? How could he have done that? He dropped his head onto the back of the couch and squeezed his eyes together even harder.

"And now this? You kiss her in front of the entire town like...like she's yours? Like you can do as you please with her? Are you trying to give your Mom a heart attack?"

"I know. I'm an idiot." He leaned forward, propping his elbows on his knees and rubbing his palms together roughly.

"Jesus, Trey. You know better than to touch a woman like that out in public. Do you want everyone to think she's just one of your weekend screws?"

"No," Trey said through gritted teeth as he rubbed his hands together harder.

"You were raised better."

"You're right!" Trey yelled, pushing himself off the couch. "You're right and I seriously messed up and she will probably never speak to me again!"

"I know I'm right. And I can only hope she never speaks to you again, but she's one of the nicest people I've ever met and has probably already forgiven you. She came here to help all of us, and you just keep screwing things up." Andy growled as he flopped down into the chair and tried to rub some of the tension from his temples. "You left her standing there, crying in front of everyone. Do you have any idea how humiliating that must have been for her? Do you even care?"

Trey's shoulders slumped and he returned to the couch. "I care."

"Well, you have one hell of a way of showing it."

Trey's words came out barely above a whisper. "She seems to be all I care about anymore. I wonder what she's doing, what she's thinking. She says things that make me think and feel and...shit, I don't know. I haven't cared about anything for so long, I don't really know what to do with all of it."

"So, you do have feelings for her?"

Several silent minutes stretched out between them.

"Did she tell you what we argued about?" Trey asked quietly.

"What do you mean?"

"In the guesthouse... Did she tell you why we were fighting?"

Andy shook his head slowly. "No, she said it wasn't important and that she had pushed you too far."

"You and Lauren."

Andy looked away, rubbing the nape of his neck with one hand.

"It's too hard," Trey's voice was soft. "I'm not sure I can do it."

"Do what, man?" Andy asked as he blew out a breath and rubbed his hands down the front of his thighs.

"Watch it happen. You two are walking around town like my brother never existed. Like what they had doesn't matter."

"Trey, it's been two and a half years. She's been alone for a long time. No one is pretending anything. Jamie and Lauren would still be happily married if he was still here. I know that, she knows that, and Alex knows it. But he's gone."

"Why does everyone feel like they have to keep reminding me of that?"

"Because you act like you keep forgetting. He's gone. And if there is one thing I know about your brother, he would never want Lauren to be alone. He would want her safe, and protected, and...loved."

Trey tried to fight against the tightness in his chest, he cleared his throat. "You love her?"

"Of course, I love her. Do you honestly think I would just mess around with someone like Lauren? She's amazing and I'm blessed by every second she wants my sorry ass around."

Trey exhaled, shifting in his seat, "Well, I would agree with the last part of that statement."

Andy smiled. "But I do love her, and God willing, I will be her husband someday. You need to be on board with that or leave us all alone to move forward without you. I won't have you causing any more trouble."

"It's so hard."

"Yep, it is," Andy agreed as he nodded his head. "I'm not going to sugarcoat it. But it's happening, and you can either be a part of it or not. Either way, it's time I stop worrying about you and concentrate on protecting Lauren, your mom, Alex...and now Callie from any more pain. And I will protect them for the rest of my life."

"Protect them from me?" Trey's eyes met Andy's, there was an honesty there that had been the foundation of years of friendship.

"Yes, from you. Right now, you're the biggest threat to this family, your family...our family."

"And Callie is part of that now?"

"She's been an amazing friend to Lauren. They have known each other for a while now and she helped Lauren through some dark days. Alex adores her and that's good enough for me." Andy stood and walked into the kitchen. He took two beers from the unopened twelve pack in the fridge. Grabbing an ice pack from the freezer, he threw it, and one of the beers at Trey as he walked back into the living room. "And let's not forget she's the one who has your mom planting flowers again, which is an absolute miracle."

"Callie is right. I am an asshole," Trey admitted as he opened his beer and pressed the ice pack to his head.

Andy laughed and raised his can in agreement, "She's a smart girl, but in this case, I have to admit you might be right too. She'd have to be a crazy person to care about you with the way you've acted." He dropped back down into the chair.

"I do care about her." Trey's heart galloped in his chest at his admission. He knew being around Callie had stirred feelings inside of him, but to admit it out loud was a whole other thing.

"I know. And that's where it starts to get complicated." Andy took another long swig of beer.

"I had Sheriff Deal do some digging around to find out who she was."

Andy sat straight up in the chair, coughing and sputtering as he wiped beer from his chin. "What? Oh shit," he leaned back and ran a hand over his face. "Why did you do that?"

Trey shrugged. "I don't know. She just showed up out of nowhere and you guys are acting all shady about it and none of you would give me any answers as to why she's here."

Andy swallowed hard and gripped his beer can harder. "And what did you find out?"

"Nothing really. Only that her name is Callie Loftier

and her daddy is a bigwig businessman on the east coast. And I know she was sick as a kid and her parents do a lot of fundraising for a pediatric hospital she grew up near. I'm guessing that's where she was treated."

Andy nodded his head, encouraging Trey to continue.

"That's really all I know. He said it was just in the beginning stages of the investigation, but even with the info I've received, I feel better."

"I'm glad you feel better, but you should be prepared, she's going to be pissed when she finds out. What the hell did you think you'd find?"

"I don't know, Andy. For all I know she was some drifter serial killer who heard about a rich, widowed farmer's wife who lives alone. She finds her on Facebook and befriends her. She shows up in the middle of a rainy night with nothing but a bag and a small, shitty car that could easily have been stolen from her last victim. She woos the whole family, makes them trust her and fall in love with her, and before you know it, everyone is dead. Crazy Girl has a pocket full of money and moves on to the next unsuspecting family."

Andy tilted his head; his eyes open wide. "First of all, woos the whole family? Have you been rereading your mama's romance books? And second, I'm not going to even comment on how detailed and creepy that story is. But I do want to mention one thing you said... fall in love with her?"

Trey's head fell back against the couch, "Shit. I'm in real trouble here."

"Uh huh," Andy agreed as he bit his bottom lip. "We're all in trouble." He took another swig of beer.

"It's just...when I'm around her I can't think rationally, you know? She makes me crazy with that sassy mouth of hers, and she's so stubborn. Don't even get me started about that whole 'free spirit' thing either because I don't understand one bit of it, but it's sexy as hell."

Trey shook his head and continued but talked more into the room than directly to Andy. "She's the exact opposite of everything I've ever been attracted to." He turned his face toward his friend. "But she's funny and kind and –"

"Beautiful."

"Yes, beautiful," Trey repeated, glaring at his friend.

Andy put his hands up in front of him, laughing out his surrender. "Just helpin' a brother out."

"I don't need any help when it comes to Callie."

"Any other woman, I would agree with you, but I've seen you with Callie. Believe me, you need some help with that girl."

Trey chuckled at the joke, but not because it wasn't right. He really did need help.

"Well," Andy said as he pushed himself to stand. "I would love to spend the night here talking about what a screw up you are, but I need to get home." Trey followed his friend to the door.

"Hey, you know it's Daisy Days this weekend, right?" Andy glanced over his shoulder as he grabbed the door handle.

"Yep, been looking forward to it all year," Trey said sarcastically.

"Your mom has decided to have her Friday night cookout."

Trey leaned against the kitchen counter and crossed his arms over his chest. "Really?"

"I think it would be really nice if you showed up. I mean, you need to apologize to Callie anyway, and plus, the old gang is coming. They would love to see you."

"I don't know, man. That's a lot to deal with." Trey dropped his eyes as he rubbed his chin.

"I get it, I really do. Baby steps."

"I'll think about it."

Andy slapped his hand onto Trey's shoulder. "But you will apologize soon, right?"

Trey pushed himself off the counter, extending his hand out toward his friend. "I will. I promise. She deserves it. Do they know you're here?"

"Shit, no!" Andy grasped his hand and shook it. "Those two women told me to stay away from you, and if you tell them I was here, I will beat your ass again."

"No way. I'd rather they don't know you were here, and for the record, I'd hardly call a couple punches through the door an ass-kicking."

"Oh yeah, O'Brien? That sure sounds like a challenge to me." Andy said jokingly, shoving Trey's shoulder.

"Save it. You'll need it for all the boys that niece of mine will have chasing her in a few short years."

"Jesus, I'm not ready to think about that." Andy shook his head, "Thanks, Trey."

"I can't say I'm one hundred percent on board, but like you said baby steps."

FIFTEEN

"Oh my God, Callie. How could you have possibly thought this was a good idea?"

Callie cringed at the panic in her sister's voice during their usual Friday phone call. She'd avoided the whole 'where are you now' conversation with Jade for the past couple of weeks, but once her sister set her mind to something, she didn't let up.

And once Callie began, the entire story of who Trey O'Brien was and what he meant to her spilled out without a filter.

"You don't understand," Callie whispered, looking down at the dark wooden porch that overlooked the backyard of the guesthouse. The sun warmed her tired legs as she took a deep breath and stretched them out in front of her. "They're losing him."

"And how is that your responsibility?"

"I don't know, Jade. It just feels like it is."

The heaviness in the silence between them was laced with an all too familiar emotion. Callie knew her sister was processing, trying to figure out one of two things. If there was some way to get Callie out of this mess, or how she was going to pick up the pieces when it was all over.

"I care about him. He's important to me. I really think I can help him get through this."

"But at what cost?"

"At whatever cost, I guess."

Jade blew out an exaggerated breath. "Oh, my Gosh, Cal! When are you going to forgive yourself for being alive?"

Callie braced herself for a conversation she and her sister had had a million times.

"You're a beautiful, thoughtful woman. You deserve to be happy. Please, what can I do to get you to come home and live your life here where you belong?"

"I am living my life." Callie closed her eyes and tried to concentrate on the sound of the birds singing. Her sister didn't understand her need to be free, but she also knew her concerns were founded in love.

"How? By floating from one place to another? By putting your physical and emotional wellbeing at risk for the sake of strangers?"

"They don't feel like strangers to me. I don't expect you to understand."

Jade sighed again, sounding annoyed. "And what about this guy's family? Don't they understand this is a potential risk for you? What if it doesn't work out and you can't save him?"

Callie shifted her weight in the chair, "I'm taking all my meds and getting plenty of rest."

"That's not what I'm talking about and you know it. This isn't your usual situation. It's so much more..." Jade paused, unsure of the right word to use.

"...personal," Callie finished.

"Yes, personal. He could really hurt you." Jade's voice cracked, and it made tears spring to Callie's eyes.

"I'm okay. I know what I'm doing. You're just going to have to trust me."

"It sounds too risky."

Callie pulled one leg up next to her and used the other to rock the chair she sat in. "Well, it is. But I knew that coming into it. My biggest fear is once he finds out the real reason I'm here, he'll feel betrayed because we didn't tell him right away. And then we'll lose him for good."

"We?" Jade questioned, but Callie couldn't find it in her to respond to that. She had no idea how to explain her feelings for Trey. Even in her own mind, it sounded frightening.

"Maybe the time has come to tell him. These things can't always be handled at the perfect time in the perfect place. Sometimes it's messy and painful, but at least everyone knows the truth. That's when people start to heal." Jade's usually comforting voice had the opposite effect tonight.

Callie squeezed the bridge of her nose and exhaled. "I don't know anything anymore except the reasons I came here are not the reasons keeping me here. Somehow, it got twisted and turned around and I just feel so out of control all the time." Her stomach churned and she pressed a hand against it, hoping to ward off the terrible feeling that had taken up residence there.

Jade's voice softened, "Isn't that what you've been looking for? The ability to lose control and not be fearful of the unknown?"

"This is different. I don't know how, but it is," Callie said.

"Or maybe this is the first time you've cared enough to let it feel different."

Moments from the time Callie had spent on the farm flashed through her mind. Images of her and Alex on her horse, Eve planting flowers, Lauren smiling at Andy. A warmth spread through her chest. It was going to be hard to leave these people. "Maybe."

"I don't have any advice for you, and I certainly have no insight because I don't know those people at all. But I'm begging you, please be careful. Take care of you first. If things get rough, come home and let me help you? Promise me that, Callie."

"I promise."

"Okay, but before you get off the phone..." Jade paused and then giggled like a teenager, "tell me about that kiss one more time."

"SO...DAISY DAYS?" Callie asked as she placed yet another stack of yellow napkins down on one of the white, cloth-covered serving tables Eve had set up in the yard. She looked toward the sky, letting the sun kiss her cheeks and enjoying the cool breeze that blew by.

Lauren laughed and Callie's heart warmed at the sound. Her friend seemed happy today. "I forget you're not a small-town girl." Lauren turned toward Callie and held up a paper plate, pointing to the daisy printed in the middle of it. "Yes, Daisy Days. Every year the whole town gets together and celebrates. The streets shut down, the music plays, and we enjoy each other's company."

"Well, okay then," Callie said, smiling at Lauren. "Sounds like I'm about to find out what small-town living is all about."

"You sure are. It used to be an O'Brien family tradition to kick off Daisy Days by having a big potluck cookout on

Friday night, but we haven't done it since Jamie died." Lauren's smile faltered for a second, but she recovered, looking back at Callie. "I'm glad Eve decided to start it up again. It's good for all of us."

It was suddenly so apparent to Callie how much she admired Lauren's strength. This woman had been to Hell and back. She could've easily given up after all the hardships in her life but here she was, fighting to keep the only family she'd ever known together and moving forward.

Callie went back to arranging the napkins, but her mind drifted to a certain O'Brien. "So, do you think he will come?"

Lauren shrugged her shoulders, "I don't know."

Callie braced herself with both hands against the table, leaning into it as she let her head hang down. "I think maybe it's time I leave."

Lauren stopped, frozen in place. "Why?"

"I just... I don't really know what to say," she squeezed her eyes together and pushed herself off the table, turning to face Lauren. "This has gotten so complicated. I feel like I've become part of the problem instead of the solution. I didn't expect Trey to be... I mean...he's so...ugh!" Callie threw the remaining napkins onto the table. "I think I might have real feelings for him, Lauren."

Lauren let out a hearty laugh, "Well, duh. That's not really a reason to leave, is it? Wouldn't that be a reason to stay?"

Callie's mouth fell open, her eyes widening as she looked at her friend. "Clearly he doesn't feel the same way."

Lauren shifted her weight to one side, lifting her eyebrows and smiling. "He kissed you, didn't he?"

Callie's nose crinkled as she crossed her arms over her chest. "He had been drinking."

"Maybe." She pointed a finger at Callie. "But I would bet Alex's horse that Trey has feelings for you." Lauren grabbed a carrot from one of the veggie plates and bit it in half, smiling at Callie as she chewed.

The screen door flew open as Eve came out carrying a case of water. Callie rushed over to help.

"Thank you." Eve took a deep breath as she lifted her chin, surveyed the yard, and placed her hands on her hips. "It's going to be a great day today. I can feel it."

Lauren began directing Andy as he pulled the biggest grill Callie had ever seen behind his truck. "Right about there," she directed. "Yep, that's perfect."

Andy leaned out his window and yelled, "Are you sure now, sweetheart, because I'm happy to move it that way six inches...and then back the other way four...just to be sure."

Lauren glared at Andy. He laughed and put his hands up in defense. "Just want to make sure it's exactly where you want it."

Eve giggled and said to Callie as she turned back toward the house, "Aren't those two the cutest?"

"That's one big grill," Callie stated after putting the bottles of water in the cooler and joining Andy and Lauren in the yard.

Lauren clapped her hands together, "This is about to be one big party."

And even though she had wished it to be true, Callie's breath hitched in her throat when Trey's truck came barreling into the driveway, coming to a stop in front of the guesthouse. He jumped out and Callie reached for Lauren's arm.

"Steady, girl," Lauren whispered, covering Callie's hand with her own.

Trey wore brown cargo shorts with a black t-shirt that

stretched across his chest and he wore a white baseball hat backward. He looked more like a larger-than-life surfer God than the moody, drunk farmer he was.

"Andy, that grill should be..."

Andy dropped his head dramatically and pointed at Lauren, letting Trey know that she's the one who had picked the spot.

"I was just saying...that spot is absolutely perfect. Exactly where I would've put it. Good job, Sis." He flashed a big smile at Lauren and winked.

Andy yelled, "Get your ass over here and help me! These women have a to-do list a mile long, and all of it has to be done before the first guest arrives."

Trey reached into the bed of his truck, pulled out a bouquet of flowers, and walked toward them. Callie suddenly struggled to breathe and her heart pounded wildly as she watched him get closer.

Eve rushed out onto the porch, her face beaming. "Oh my goodness, you're here!" She looked over at Callie and Lauren, "See, girls, I told you this was going to be a great day."

Eve stepped off the porch, setting down a plate of food and meeting her son in front of the tables. "Trey, can you help Andy bring around the bales of hay from the barn and set them around the food areas so people have extra seating?"

"Well hello to you too, Mom," he said teasingly as he presented the flowers to his mom.

Eve paused, taking the flowers from her son and smiling brightly. "Thank you, sweet boy," she said as she raised up on her toes to kiss him on the cheek. "I'm so glad you're here."

"It feels good to be here," Trey admitted.

Eve's eyes filled with tears, but she shook them away. "I need to get these in some water," she said as she inhaled deeply. "You guys get to work. The first guests should be arriving any time now."

Callie moved back over to the table she had been working on and began fidgeting with the napkins, trying to hide her trembling hands. She was sure everyone in the county could hear her heart thundering inside of her chest. She tried to ignore him, tried to be unaffected, but in the span of a heartbeat, she remembered it all.

How it felt when her body melted into his, and how safe he'd made her feel when they'd shared their dance in the rain. The way he always stood a little too close, invading her space and making it his. How he somehow looked even more handsome covered in dirt after working on the farm all day. His scent that surrounded her, claiming her, and making her stomach clench with excitement. The way his eyes twinkled when he was about to tease her. The smile that could light up an entire room. The desperation in their kiss and the way he'd whispered to her afterward.

"Hey," Trey said as he appeared next to her.

One word. He had only spoken one word, yet the sound of his soft voice slid over her skin like silk while leaving a fiery trail at the same time. Every part of her was acutely aware of every part of him.

"Hey," she responded, a bit too friendly and without turning around.

He reached out and touched her elbow and she stilled. Nothing else mattered except where they were connected. She watched as his fingers slid down her arm, stopping on the top of her hand where he rubbed small circles, all the while she tried to remember how to breathe. "Can I talk to you for a second?"

She pulled in a shaky breath and turned, keeping her eyes on the ground.

A surge of panic raced through Trey. He wanted her eyes on him, wanted her to see the apology, not just hear it. Guilt squeezed his chest, stealing his breath for a second, and he sent a promise up to his brother that he would never stop trying to make up for losing his cool with her.

Since the moment he'd found out she had been sick as a child, something inside of him had shifted. He'd finally realized why she'd come here.

He could only imagine how scared Callie must have been as a small child, facing illness, and for all he knew, death. How hard that must've been for her. She was a survivor in the real sense of the word and she was helping his mom and Lauren be survivors, too.

Somewhere in the darkness of the night, as he'd laid in bed after finding out the information Sheriff Deal had given him, he realized she wasn't only there to help them deal with the loss of Jamie, she was also there to help them prepare for the loss of him.

Callie had been right all along, he was an idiot.

The comments she made the first morning she woke him up, about choosing to stay in the guesthouse with his alcohol instead of spending time with his family. The conversation in the truck about what he felt was the definition of security. The horrible argument they'd had in the guesthouse about letting Lauren move on, and still, after that, Callie had pleaded with him in the grocery store to talk with his mom.

She had given life back to this farm. Callie was the reason his mom had started living again. She was the source of strength for Lauren and Andy to admit their feelings for each other.

And he had done nothing but blame and hurt her.

He couldn't explain it, but he knew it had changed him and he needed her to feel that change, too.

But he did want to push her. Things seemed different today, she seemed different.

He pulled the two daisies out from behind his back and held them down low so she could see them. Callie's lips lifted into a small smile as she slowly took the flowers and raised her eyes to him. He knew at that moment, there was nothing more beautiful in this world than this woman. He swallowed past the lump in his throat. "I'm really sorry, Callie."

Her smile fell and so did his heart. He didn't want to remember either, but they had to get through this. They couldn't leave what had happened just hanging out there. There was something about her that kept him coming back, and he needed her to understand no matter what, no matter how hard things got, that would never change. He needed her to trust in that. But first, he needed her to forgive him. Her forgiveness would be the foundation they could start building from.

"For what?" She asked as she took in a deep breath that filled both of her lungs full, and somehow, she found the courage to lift her gaze to him once again.

She could see the desperation as he searched her face, his eyes filled with such pain and suffering. Her heart swelled with hope that maybe he needed her, as much as she had come to realize that she needed him. This could work if they both wanted it. Sure, the truth would change things a bit, but for the better. It could make them closer and she was willing to work through all the obstacles that it might bring.

"I don't really know where to start. What can I say to make you understand how sorry I am?"

"Trey –"

"No, please, let me finish. First, that day in the guest-house, when I..." he dropped his eyes to the ground and shook his head, pursing his lips together. "When I pushed you. God, Callie. You will never know how sorry I am for that. I crossed every single line a man should have with a woman, and even if you somehow find it in your heart to forgive me, I want you to know that I will never forgive myself."

He ran his hands down his face. "And for not trusting you. For jumping to conclusions."

Callie shook her head, it was all okay. She understood he was hurting and finally feeling emotions that he had suppressed for so long. It was natural for him to be suspicious. She reached for him as he began pacing.

"And that kiss, it should've never happened. That was horrible."

Callie held her breath, feeling like someone had punched her in the stomach as her head swirled. The sting of his words cutting through her heart like a knife. Her throat constricted and she turned away, not wanting him to see the hurt on her face.

Sure, this was a new beginning. But not for the two of them together. This was a new beginning for him. He was starting a new life, the life she wanted for him. A life recon-nected with his family, and free from the pain he had self-inflicted. She had been such a silly girl to think someone like Trey would want a beginning with her.

He needed her forgiveness so he could move on. Without her. And she decided in that moment she cared enough for him to give him just that.

Callie waved her hand in the air. "It's no big deal. You're forgiven." She said as she maneuvered around the table and headed toward the guesthouse. "I need to put these in water," she echoed what Eve had said just minutes ago, hoping it would give her the same reprieve.

"Just like that?" He yelled after her.

"Yup, just like that." She hurried toward the guesthouse.

Trey put his hands on top of his head, chewing his bottom lip as he watched Callie rush away from him. He took a few quick steps toward her before Andy stepped in front of him.

"Whoa, let's take a moment here," Andy suggested as he placed a hand on Trey's chest.

Trey looked down at Andy's hand, and then back up to his face.

"You think I'm going to hurt her again?"

"Jesus, no, Trey. But I also know if you go rushing in there like this, it's not going to go well."

"How the hell do you know that?"

"Well, I don't know. How did that just go?" He pointed to the spot where Trey and Callie had just been standing.

"Shitty." Trey took a step back from Andy and began pacing again.

"Yeah, that's what I thought. It seemed a little too easy."

"What is my problem? I can't do anything right with this girl. My words don't come out right, my thoughts get all jumbled up in my head. I'm constantly saying and doing stupid shit when she's around."

Andy threw his head back laughing.

"This is funny to you? What if she can't forgive me, Andy? I basically called her a liar and a fake. I invaded her space, hurt her, and then took advantage of her kindness when all she was trying to do, all she's ever tried to do, is knit me back into this family."

"First of all, I don't think it's funny. I think it's hilarious! I've never seen you so bent over a girl. Welcome to the real world, O'Brien."

Trey flipped a finger in the air toward his friend.

"Secondly, all I'm saying is dial it down a notch. You can't go in there all wound up. Take a breath and think about it. Callie isn't the type of girl you go after and then throw away. You have to be sure because she will see through the usual crap that works on other girls."

"I would love to stroke your ego here and tell you that's a great idea, but the reality of it is this, I'm Trey O'Brien. I don't dial anything down and I have no intention of throwing her away."

"So, you've decided to stick around then? Be a part of this family again?"

"I'll tell you what I've decided," Trey pointed in the direction of the guesthouse. "That woman is going to be mine, and I'll do whatever it takes to make sure she knows it."

Andy started laughing, "Sounds like you."

Trey smiled and slapped Andy on the shoulder as he started after Callie. "You know those baby steps we talked about? I say screw that."

SIXTEEN

CALLIE PULLED OPEN THE SCREEN DOOR AND DIDN'T stop until she was in the security of the kitchen. She pressed the flowers against her chest as it rose and fell quickly.

"Callie?"

The sound of his voice was like a call to action as she opened the cupboard in front of her, rummaging through the cups and plates, pretending to be looking for something to put the flowers in. "Yes?"

"Can I come in?"

She panicked because there was nothing in the stupid cupboard to put the flowers in. Everything was either too small or too big or just not right. She quickly moved to the next one. "Um, yeah, sure. Whatever, it's your house."

She didn't turn toward the sound of the screen door opening. The world tilted a little bit and dizziness filled her head. His soft voice reached into her, squeezing her heart. "Yeah, but your space, remember?"

She closed her eyes, dropping her chin down as she ran a hand up and over her forehead and down her ponytail. "Right..."

Callie finally turned around. He was close, too close, but she couldn't seem to make herself move back. The only space left between them was the flowers he had given her. She tightened her grip, needing something to keep her grounded. She had known his touch, had felt his hands on her during their dance, but now that she knew the warm feel of her rushed breath mixed with his and the taste of his lips on hers, there was nothing that could stop the desire for more.

But he had said it, the kiss was a mistake. Something he regretted.

She had her answer. Her sister was right, she needed to be selfish right now, think about herself and her own wellbeing. For the first time since her surgery, she wanted to go home.

Panic rose inside of her like a tidal wave, swirling and swaying. Her stomach rolled, and she tried desperately to keep in control. She didn't want to be pulled under this time, she wanted to live and continue on. But Callie knew she belonged to this man, even if he didn't want her, and it was heartbreaking to realize sometimes loving someone just isn't enough.

He leaned in closer, his scent surrounding her and stealing her breath. She fought everything within herself not to drop the flowers in her hands and wrap her arms around him. He reached above the refrigerator and opened the cupboard, grabbing a small vase and handing it to her as he took a step back.

"Thanks," she mumbled and turned toward the sink.

He leaned against the counter, crossing his arms over his chest and looking out the windows.

"I've been a huge asshole to you."

She snuck a sideways glance at him but only for a few

seconds. She knew if she spent any longer than that, she would fall under his spell once again. "It's okay. I guess I gave you a reason to wonder, showing up like I did." Callie rushed past him and onto the back porch, setting the vase with the flowers down on the table.

"I have to tell you something," he said, following her.

She turned to face him standing in the doorway, hoping the hurricane of emotions she was dealing with on the inside wouldn't be plastered all over her face.

"I know why you're here," he said calmly.

Callie's stomach threatened to spill her breakfast, but she tried to keep her voice as light as possible.

"You do?"

"Don't be angry, but I had someone checking into you."

Callie stiffened, "What?"

Trey put his hands up in defense and continued. "I know you're Callie Loftier. I know your daddy is a big deal and sells shipping supplies on the coast."

This was it, he really did know. Callie prepared herself. She was going to tell Trey the truth, right here, right now, and all by herself. Goosebumps broke out all over her body and she couldn't make herself look at him. But if this is the way fate had set it up, then who was she to fight it? She could tell him and leave. Pack up her clothes and be gone before the first person even arrived at the party.

"And I know you are really sick."

Callie grabbed the railing to steady herself. "Was," she whispered.

"What?"

She turned toward him again, her resolve and strength returning as she remembered all the things she had been through to get her to this moment. "I was really sick, I'm not sick now. That's not who I am anymore."

"It's not who you ever were. You were never your illness, Callie. It might have been part of who you were, but it was never who you were."

"How could you possibly know that? You have no idea what it's like to be me." She turned, determined to get away from all of this, but Trey grabbed her arm lightly so she would look at him.

"You're right, I don't."

"And? What does all this newfound information about me tell you?"

"When I first met you, I assumed you had found my mom on some gardening website. Found out who she was and that she had...well, that she had money, and maybe you would show up and somehow take advantage of her."

"Oh, that's what you thought?"

"Yes, I thought that."

"And what do you think now?"

"I think you needed her as much as she needed you."

Callie felt her strength wavering. This man. This man and his damn words and his perfect smile and his beautiful soul. "What do you mean?" she asked, her voice cracking as she spoke.

"It means I know she is hurting and grieving, even more than me. I've been too damn selfish to see it because I was so caught up in my own self-pity."

Callie wanted to scream, this was taking too long. She needed to tell him the truth now before she lost her nerve. But she also understood he needed this time to say everything he wanted. This was important to his healing.

"I remember her telling me about a group she found online. Crossing Bridges, or Mending Bridges, something like that."

"Building Bridges," Callie said carefully.

"Yes, that's it," Trey said, pointing toward Callie. "That's the group you met in, right?"

Callie nodded her head.

"She told me it was a group where people who are dealing with serious illnesses can talk to people who have lost loved ones. It's sort of like a therapy group, right?"

"Trey..."

"I mean... I still think it's kind of strange you guys decided to meet in person, but at least now I know the reasons behind it. What I'm getting at is this... I was wrong. I don't think that about you anymore and I was really hoping we could just start over?"

"What?" A long silence stretched between them.

"I want to start over," he pushed his hand in Callie's direction. "I'm Trey O'Brien, Eve's youngest son, and I'm pleased to meet you."

She hesitated, knowing there was so much more to be said, but his eyes were so hopeful, and her heart couldn't deny him this little victory. "Hi," she said as she smiled, reaching for his hand.

As soon as his hand closed over hers, he pulled her to him, their bodies touching while he pressed her hand over his heart. "Do you feel that? Do you feel how crazy you make my heart beat when I'm close to you?"

His other hand traced down the curve of her body, finding her hip and pulling her in closer if that was even possible. Electrical currents rushed around her body, sending a shiver down her back. Callie grasped his t-shirt, unsure if her weakening knees would keep her standing without help. He leaned down, his lips hovering just over the shell of her ear as his hot breath bathed her sensitive skin. "Hi," he whispered huskily, and she could feel him smile against her ear.

She turned her face towards him, breathless and weak from his nearness. There was a heavy silence as their breaths tangled between them, their eyes finding each other, silently questioning how far each would let this go. "That's some greeting," Callie said, smiling. "Is this how you say hello to everyone?"

Trey laughed, a real laugh and Callie had never heard anything so beautiful. "No, this is a new one for me." Trey took a small step back and Callie started to release his shirt, but he quickly put a hand over hers, keeping it next to his heart. She didn't want to let go, every cell in her body wanted to be tucked back in next to him, and her heart warmed knowing he wasn't ready for her to let go yet either.

Trey kept his eyes on where their hands met on his chest. A small smirk lifted the corner of his mouth as he spoke, "And for the record, I don't dance either."

Callie's lips parted as his eyes found hers.

"I don't dance, ever. Only with you. This is all new to me, Cal." He lifted her hand to his lips and kissed it gently. "People should be coming soon, I better get out there and help Andy."

"Of course," she said breathlessly, his words breaking through the trance she was in. She gently pulled her hand from his and took a step back. "I'm just going to change and freshen up and I'll be right out to help."

"Why? I think you look awesome in what you're wearing."

Callie looked down at her old shoes she wore whenever she worked in the dirt, her black silky running shorts with a white stripe down the side, and her favorite "Johanns Sweet Corn" t-shirt she picked up somewhere in Iowa that read, *Put Johanns up if you love our sweet corn.*

She did love that sweet corn.

"Well thanks, but I think I'll change into something a little nicer if I'm going to meet the whole town."

Trey smiled, "Whatever makes you happy. I guess I'll see you out there," he said, pointing with his thumb over his shoulder, "unless you need some help getting ready."

Callie rolled her eyes, "Do those pick-up lines work on the girls around here?"

"Sometimes."

"Well, not today, farmer."

SEVENTEEN

The party was well underway when Callie finally forced herself from the guesthouse. She didn't have a reason to carry many clothes with her and a party was something she wasn't prepared for... especially like the one going on outside, with loud music and the smell of grilled hamburger floating through the air.

She had settled on a light pink, button-up sundress. Even though it was warm out, she left her hair down, letting it air-dry after her shower. It flowed in perfect beach waves down her back. She slipped on her trusty flip-flops and a dab of lip gloss and called it good. It was casual, but she was comfortable and that's all she cared about.

As soon as her feet hit the gravel of the driveway, she stopped. Most of the guys were dressed one of two ways; the younger ones were dressed exactly like Trey, with slight variations, and the older ones wore jeans with cowboy boots and a western-style shirt

The girls her age, however, were a bit shocking to Callie. Most wore tight tank tops. Some layered them, some topped them off with a denim shirt, but almost all of them had on short shorts and cowboy boots. It was like a light shone down on her, pointing out to everyone how badly she didn't belong here.

"This looks like a county music video gone bad," she whispered to herself. Callie wanted to turn and run back into the guesthouse, hide out until everyone left, and head out of town at first light.

In her mind, she had already decided that was the best plan of action. Callie had initially agreed to stay until this all played out, but the rules had changed. She had never intended for Trey to be misled or lied to. That wasn't how this was supposed to go. She meant to come to the O'Brien farm, put a plan into motion, see it through, and leave. Just like she had with all the other families. She never intended to stay this long, play these sorts of games, or feel the way she did when Trey whispered her name.

This was a horrible time to tell Eve she was leaving, and she felt terrible about that, but she couldn't disappear without telling her. She knew if she didn't do it tonight, she would probably end up living in the guesthouse for the rest of her life. She couldn't let that happen. She had made a promise to herself to never be tied to one spot again. The idea of it made her anxious and she fought the sudden feeling of heaviness in her chest.

She spotted Eve across the yard and began weaving her way through the crowd. People were friendly, nodding and saying hello, but she still felt like the outsider she knew she was.

"Well, hello, beautiful," Eve said as she approached. She motioned to a woman standing in a group of ladies just a few feet away. "Joslyn, ladies, come here. I want you to meet someone."

The ladies all moved as a group, hugging their kooziewrapped beer cans, and smiling through red painted lips. Callie recognized some of the women from the day at the farmer's market.

"Ladies, this is Callie." Eve wrapped her arm around Callie's shoulders and gave her a squeeze. "The one I was telling you about. She's the one who brought this farm back to life."

All the women smiled warmly at her, thanking her for getting Eve back into the dirt.

"Callie, these gals are from the Worth County Gardening Club." Eve leaned in toward her, "They are my tribe as all you girls say."

"So nice to meet you all. I hope you're having a nice time." Callie wrung her hands together in front of her, trying her best to act like she was hearing every word when all she could hear was the steadily increasing heartbeat pounding away in her chest.

"O'Brien parties are always the best," said the woman Eve had referred to as Joslyn. Callie just smiled. "And to see Trey here, well, it's nothing less than a miracle. Isn't that right Eve?"

Eve nodded her head, looking out over the crowd toward where Trey was sitting on a hay bale enjoying the conversation with his friends. "Look at him," Eve said, tears welling up in her eyes. "He's actually smiling."

Callie followed Eve's stare and was instantly mesmerized by all things Trey. He was smiling. A real smile that lit up his face and if possible made him even more beautiful. People were all around him, laughing and patting him on the back. It was apparent that everyone was happy to have him back.

Her secret could make this all come crashing down once again.

And then she knew, she would never get the chance to love him. The pain in her chest caught her off guard, making her gasp for air.

Joslyn spoke again, pulling back Callie's fractured attention. "And I hear we also have you to thank for breathing life back into that boy."

Callie looked at Joslyn's smile and it felt like the entire world was crashing down around her. Her cheeks warmed, and she choked on the words coming out of her mouth.

"Oh, I'm not so sure about that." She rubbed her neck, trying to relieve the tension. "Eve, could I talk to you for a minute, please?" She needed to leave now. She knew it was cowardly and leaving Eve and the rest of them to handle the fall out was the last thing she wanted to do. But she was fading fast and her sister was right, this was going to destroy her. Her mind was suddenly filled with racing thoughts:

This was not her family and she had done nothing wrong to get herself to this day.

This was not her family.

She was not to blame for this.

This was not her family.

This was not her responsibility.

Trey was not hers.

The world began to tilt. Her breathing was rushed and shallow.

"Sure, honey. Can you go into the kitchen and grab those extra forks from the table and I'll be right in?"

"Sorry, Mama, I've been waiting to show this pretty lady off. Do you mind if I steal her?" Trey teased as he slipped an arm around Callie's waist. She leaned into him, taking a slow deep breath.

"Oh no, you guys go. I can get my own forks," Eve said as she and her friends smiled.

"Come on," Trey whispered, threading his fingers through hers and pulling her behind him.

Trey pulled Callie around the corner of the house. "Are you okay? You look half scared to death."

Callie tried to speak but her dry throat made it nearly impossible. She looked back toward where the party was going on. "It's just... a lot of people," she managed to get out just above a whisper.

"Do you want to leave? We could go down to my house and get away from all of this craziness."

Callie glanced toward the group of Trey's friends who had waited so long for this day.

She shook her head and took a step away from him. She needed to break this connection and now was a good time to start. This time tomorrow she would be gone, so there was no reason to encourage his interest. "No, I'm okay. Really. I just needed a breather and now I feel much better." She forced herself to look up at him with a small smile.

His eyebrows pulled together as he tilted his head examining her. "Do you want to meet some of my friends?"

"Sure," she answered, knowing she had to get away from Trey, and adding more people to the mix would make that easier. She walked out from behind the house and Trey followed.

"Everyone..." they all stopped and every single one of them looked right at her. This is not at all what she was prepared for. She had hoped for quiet introductions to individual people as she walked through the crowd and made her way over to Lauren. She should've known Trey would make a big announcement. "I would like you all to meet Callie. Callie, this is everyone."

The few seconds of awkward silence set Callie's nerves on fire. Every eye was on her as she struggled to stay standing. She smiled and waved shyly. And suddenly there was a collective greeting as people waved back, lifted their drinks toward her, and called out "Hi, Callie!"

"Hello, there." Callie jumped as a very handsome, dark-haired man appeared in front of her and stretched out his hand. "My name is Jesse and I have known this loser since we were in grade school. Now, what makes a pretty, little thing like yourself want to hang around a guy like this?" Jesse was not as tall as Trey but just as impressive in size. His light brown eyes against his tan skin were breathtaking and Callie couldn't help but think how lucky the girls in this town were. *If I grew up surrounded by men that looked like Jesse and Trey, I'd settle down, get married, and start having babies right away, too.*

"Oh, no. I'm not with... I just came to help his mom with the flowers."

"Really?" Jesse stretched the word out like it was a tease. "So, you and –"

"Back off, Jess. Give the girl some room," Lauren said from behind him. He took a step to the side, letting Lauren through. She linked arms with Callie and led her away from an obviously irritated Trey and a satisfied Jesse who was very pleased with himself.

"Just breathe. You look like you're about to pass out," Lauren whispered, and she walked her over to another couple.

"This is Ginnie O'Brien. She is a cousin and lives one town over."

She smiled warmly at Callie, "I hear you're staying in the guesthouse. That place is beautiful, isn't it? I remember when the boys were working on it with Uncle Jed. It was the talk of the entire county!"

"It's like nothing I've ever seen before," Callie spoke

truthfully.

"And this is Chad Turnfell. His wife is over there chasing their twin toddlers around."

Chad tipped his hat at Callie but quickly added, "Nice to meet you, Callie. Don't mean to be rude, but I'm afraid if I don't get over there to help my wife, I won't be around for another harvest season." Callie smiled and watched as he ran to help his exhausted-looking wife.

"His daddy and Jed went to high school together, and he played football with the boys," Lauren explained as she handed Callie a bottle of water.

"Did you grow up with all of these people?" Callie asked as her eyes scanned the crowd.

There was a familiarity between all of them that she was unaccustomed to. She had never experienced anything like it. She had her parents and her sister – that was it. Most of her past was spent in the hospital or the beach house. A sheen of sweat broke out on her forehead.

Lauren smiled as she looked over the crowd of people fanned out around them. "Most of them, yes. Some went away to college and brought back husbands or wives, but for the most part, these are the people who have been in our lives for as long as I can remember."

This is his life. Callie thought. This is what he's missing. She took a quick drink of her water, trying to swallow past the huge lump in her throat.

"Are you sure you're feeling okay?" Lauren worried as she led Callie to a seat. "I'm going to get you something to eat," she said. "I think you've been working yourself too hard." Callie wanted to tell her no, but she couldn't find the words. Instead, she spotted Trey sitting across from her. She watched him... and he watched her, sending small smiles whenever he could catch her eye.

Lauren returned with a plate of food just as Chad came back with a brown-haired little boy tucked under his arm. "So, Trey... You going to be around to take over second base tomorrow?"

Trey shook his head as he looked at the ground. "Haven't played for a long time, man."

"Come on! We sure could use your glove tomorrow. This is our last year in the young men's bracket and to tell you the truth, we might have our hands full with that college-aged team this year. Man, they have some strong boys on that team."

Callie looked at Lauren, confused by this conversation as she took another sip of water. "Every year the guys play in a softball tournament. It's a fundraiser to buy supplies for the elementary school kids." She raised her voice so everyone could hear, "It's supposed to be a charity tournament, but these yahoos treat it like the World Series playoffs."

"Yes, he's playing." Jesse chimed in as he sat next to Trey on the hay bale. "Lauren, you know as well as anyone else, how important bragging rights are when it comes to this tournament. We have a four-year run and we aren't about to lose it!"

"This is Caleb Williams and his beautiful wife, Becca." Lauren introduced as the couple walked over. "They stood up with Jamie and me in our wedding and we did the same for them. Caleb was Jamie's best friend." Lauren looked at Callie as if she should understand what she was implying. They knew. They knew the truth of why she was here.

Callie's eyes filled with tears as she stood and reached out for Becca's hand first and then Caleb's next, "So nice to meet you guys."

Caleb wrapped his big hand around Callie's. Talking in

a hushed tone, he said, "We are so happy you're here with us. I know it might be a little strange, but it makes us feel like a little part of Jamie is here with us."

She forced a smile, nodding once at Caleb.

Her eyes shot over to Trey and once again, he smiled at her. That's all it took for Callie to completely lose control. The rushing thoughts returned with a vengeance. This is his life. He should be here. I don't belong here. This could never be my life. This will never be my life.

Callie dropped Caleb's hand and took a few steps backward. "Lauren, I have to... I don't feel so well." Knowing she had to slow her breathing, she turned toward the guesthouse.

In 1, 2, 3... out 1, 2, 3... she counted in her head, trying to slow her breathing. In 1, 2, 3... his life... out 2, 3. In 2, 3... not mine... out 2, 3.

"Trey? Trey, you better get over here!" Lauren shouted. "Callie, sweetheart? Are you okay?"

Caleb led Callie back to where she'd been sitting before. "Just sit down, darlin', everything will be okay."

"Callie, what's wrong?" Trey asked worriedly, kneeling in front of her.

"It's all wrong," she said as she grabbed his hands, squeezing them tightly.

"You need to slow your breathing or you're going to pass out," Andy encouraged from behind Trey. She looked toward him and froze. Everyone stood behind him. Watching her, waiting to see what was going to happen.

"Callie, baby, can you hear me?" He sounded like he was a million miles away. She blinked slowly as she returned her gaze to him.

"Lauren, go get Dr. Johnson. I think he's down by the barn," Trey ordered.

"In 2, 3... not my life... out 2, 3. In 2, 3... he should be here, out 2, 3," she repeated.

"Shh, it's okay. I'm here."

Callie's vision began to blur and she clutched onto Trey even harder.

"Screw this." Trey slipped one arm under her shoulders and one under her knees.

"Jess! Andy!" he barked.

"Right behind you," Jesse responded as the three of them ran toward the guesthouse.

Jesse sprinted ahead of them, yanking open the door. Trey ran inside, yelling for someone to get the doctor and his mom before taking the steps to the loft two at a time until he was at the edge of the bed.

Andy followed him up with a wet washcloth and a glass of water.

"Doc is running across the yard now and your Mom is on his heels," Jesse hollered from below.

"What the hell happened?" Andy asked.

"I don't know, but she was mumbling something about this not being her life. What do you suppose that means?"

CALLIE STRETCHED, feeling like she'd been hit by a truck. She grimaced, her head pounding like someone had taken a hammer to her head. She rolled to the side, groaning as she pushed against her temples.

"Callie? Are you okay?"

She blinked several times, trying to focus her eyes, even though she knew that voice.

She pushed herself into a sitting position as she scooted

herself back toward the headboard. Trey stood, tucking pillows behind her.

"Thanks," she said softly as he handed her some Tylenol and a glass of water from the bedside table.

"How are you feeling?"

She downed the pills and he took the glass from her. She sighed deeply, "Stupid."

"What? Why?"

"I know what happened, Trey. I've had panic attacks my entire life."

"But I don't understand why you feel stupid."

"The very first time I meet all these people in your life, and I shut down like some sort of social outcast."

"Stop it," he scolded as he sat down on the edge of the bed next to her.

"No, seriously, listen to me," she grabbed his hands and he laced his fingers with hers. "What you have with those people..." she swallowed hard, "what your brother had with them..." Trey's eyes found hers, "That's special. Not everyone gets that. I know it's your normal but believe me, it's something that most people dream of but never actually get. You need to cherish those relationships. Promise me. Promise me you'll do that."

Trey swallowed hard and nodded his head. "I will, I promise."

She fell back against the headboard, blinking slowly. "Good. That's a good thing."

Suddenly the smell of food wafted its way to her nose and her stomach growled.

Trey chuckled, "Are you hungry?"

"I guess I am," she confessed, grabbing at her middle section and blushing.

Trey held out a hand to her. "Well, come on. Some people are waiting for you."

She accepted his hand and pulled herself up and off the bed. She tried to straighten her wild hair but ended up grabbing a band and pulling it up into a messy bun.

When they reached the steps, Callie came to a halt. They were all there – Jesse, Andy, Lauren, even Caleb and Becca. They were in the living room, talking in hushed voices.

"Why are they here?" she asked quietly, taking a step back, trying to avoid being seen. She wasn't that hungry.

"The princess is awake," Jesse announced, and she knew there was no hiding now. She stepped closer to the stairs and forced a smiled as Jesse raised a beer bottle in her direction.

Trey lowered his head and whispered in her ear, "They're here for you. They wanted to make sure you were okay."

Lauren rushed to the bottom of the stairs, "Callie, are you feeling better?"

Callie managed another smile, more to make Lauren feel better than to actually reflect how she was feeling, "I'm much better. Sorry if I scared you," she gave Lauren a hug when she reached the bottom. "Sorry everyone...really. I didn't mean to ruin the party."

"You ruined nothing, sweetheart," Jesse said before he took a big swig of beer, "It's about time someone showed up and made life around here a bit more exciting." He wrapped a heavy arm around her, "I'm glad you're okay though."

Becca had already begun to take pans out of the oven and set them on the island while Lauren dug in the refrigerator.

"Who's hungry?"

EIGHTEEN

CALLIE FOLLOWED LAUREN UP THE METAL BLEACHERS toward the group of women waiting for them.

"Hi, ladies. We've saved you a spot," Becca said as she pointed down to a brightly colored quilt that was laying across the seats.

"Is it supposed to get cold?" Callie asked as she helped Alex up the bleachers with one hand while trying to hold onto the large drink and popcorn that Lauren had insisted she buy at the concession stand.

"No, but you'll be grateful for that blanket soon enough." Callie gave her a confused look and Lauren laughed. "Just sit and enjoy yourself."

Callie did as she was told and Alex plopped down between the two of them, helping herself to a handful of Callie's popcorn.

"Hey, hey!" Alex shouted excitedly, jumping up and down in her seat and waving frantically. "There he is! There he is! Hi, Uncle Trey!"

"Hey, Firefly," Trey said as he came up to the fence right in front of them.

"Look! Look at me! I'm your number one fan!" She turned around and proudly displayed his number and the name O'Brien on the back of her home-made t-shirt.

"Well, well... You are the prettiest girl to wear that name since your mama wore your daddy's football jersey back in high school."

"Yep, that's about right," Alex stated confidently as she grabbed a handful of popcorn.

"Hey, are you eating all my popcorn?" he laughed as he watched the young girl shove a handful into her mouth.

"Nope, I'm eating all of Callie's, but I'm sure she'd get you something if you'd like."

Trey's eyes fixated on Callie and he lifted his chin in her direction, a smirk on his face. "Hey, Cal. Glad you could make it."

Callie shifted in her seat, heating under his pointed stare. She grabbed a handful of popcorn, shoving it into her mouth as she looked away, "Hey," she mumbled quickly.

Lauren giggled next to her.

"Do you want some popcorn or not?" Alex asked.

"No, I'm fine sweetie."

"Okay then, good luck," Alex said, giving her uncle two thumbs up.

He winked and turned away.

"Oh wait, Uncle Trey? I heard a bunch of ladies talking at the concession stand about how hot you looked in your pants. Maybe you should change into shorts so you're not so hot."

The entire bleachers roared with laughter, and Callie thought for a second, she had seen a slight blush on Trey's cheeks.

"Thanks, Firefly. I'll think about it."

After 5 hours of watching slow pitch softball, it was

finally over. They hadn't won the tournament but they all seemed to be happy with second place. Callie had no idea that baseball was so sexy. All the running and rolling in the dirt. She almost couldn't watch Trey play because he was the hottest thing she'd ever seen when he was clean but dirty...she almost couldn't take it.

"Now what?" Callie asked as she stood stretching out her legs and bending the stiffness out of her back.

"Well, now we take that little one to the lock-in and we get ready for the street dance," she informed as she pointed toward Alex who was running around with a gang of girls her age.

"Street dance?"

"Yep, that's why they have Main Street closed off. The band starts at seven and plays until ten. After that, there are fireworks at the edge of town."

"I could stay home with Alex, then you wouldn't have to pay for a sitter," she said as Alex and her friends walked up.

"What? Are you crazy? Sorry, Callie but I'm going to my own party." Alex beamed and all the little girls around her nodded their heads.

"What am I missing here?"

"Every year on Daisy Days, the youth group from our church has a lock-in. They invite all the kids from town and have games and food and chaperones, and I swear they have more fun than any of us do. The kids spend the night at the church and they feed them breakfast. It's a great way to keep the kids safe and not have to worry about them while the adults are out having adult fun." Lauren flashed Callie a huge smile.

"Sounds like a blast, but I'm not much of a dancer so I wouldn't be any fun tonight." She didn't like to lie to

Lauren, but this would give her the opportunity to pack up and leave without anyone noticing. It was the perfect cover.

"Callie Loftier," Trey hollered as he and Jesse walked up. "What are you saying? You're going to miss out on the best 80's cover band that Worth County has ever heard? You can't be serious." He put his hand over his heart and winced like it was breaking.

"It's going to be tons of fun." Jesse gave her a big smile. "You have to come."

And as if sensing her uneasiness, Alex grabbed ahold of Callie's hand and pulled her away from the crowd. "Or you could come to the church with me and hang out. You'll be the oldest one there that isn't a chaperone, but my friends will all be nice to you. They all think you're beautiful. You can sleep next to me on the floor and I'll even let you use my Wonder Woman sleeping bag."

Callie bent down to Alex's level and pushed a blonde curl behind her ear. "Wonder Woman, huh? Geesh, that's pretty tempting." Callie took a deep breath and tapped her finger on her cheek dramatically.

"I just don't think I should crash your party before I officially meet your friends. I mean, I want their first impression of me to be a good one. So, I guess I better go with your mom and Uncle Trey to the street dance."

Alex reached over and patted Callie's cheek with her little girl hand, "I think that's a good decision." She turned toward the others, "She's decided to go with the adults."

Everyone started laughing and Trey picked up his niece, tickling her until she squirmed in his arms. She puffed her cheeks out as she held her breath and tried not to laugh.

"Thanks for settling that for us." He set her back on her feet and her hands instantly went to her hips.

"Uncle Trey, you stink." She pointed one finger at him while she used the other hand to pinch her nose closed. "You need to go home and shower mister, because you are not fit to be around people."

He bent down, arms open wide as if he was going to scoop her up. She let out a little yelp when she realized his intentions and took off running, her uncle close on her heels. "But I thought you were my biggest fan!" he yelled after her. "Come and give your uncle another hug."

Trey chased Alex all the way to Lauren's SUV and made sure she was buckled in tight. Then came around and knocked on Callie's window.

"Hey, Cal?"

"What's up?"

"I was wondering if I could pick you up for the dance?" His smile was a bit shy, almost like he was afraid to ask her.

She squirmed in her seat. "Um, I guess that would be okay," she replied before she could process what her answer was.

He tapped the top of the SUV, "Great, I'll pick you up at seven?"

She nodded and he winked at her, smiling like he had after hitting that home run in game two.

"'Bye O'Brien girls. Love you."

Lauren and Callie both stared, dazed as Trey walked toward his truck.

"What was that?" Lauren asked in a hushed whisper.

"I have no idea," Alex whispered from the back seat, pulling Lauren and Callie from their fog.

Lauren reached for the DVD player and pushed play on Alex's current favorite movie.

She waited until Alex was fully engaged with the movie before speaking again.

"It was like he was the old Trey. Before Jamie died."

Callie just shook her head, looking wide-eyed at Lauren as they drove down the road.

"I don't know. It's like he's flipped a switch."

"Right? It's strange. I should be happy, I mean...I am happy but, I just don't want to trust it," Lauren fretted.

"I think I need to leave."

"Why do you keep saying that?"

"I don't know. What if this has something to do with me being here."

"What do you mean if? I think it's time you accept the fact that Trey's turnaround has everything to do with you being here."

The two sat in a weighted silence as The Princess Bride played from the back seat.

"He needs to know the truth," Callie affirmed, unable to look up from her hands.

"I know. The longer we let this go on, the harder it will be to tell him."

"I need to leave, or we need to tell him, and then I leave."

"Why would you need to leave if we tell him the truth?"

"Do you honestly think he's going to want anything to do with me?"

A shriek from the back seat made Callie jump. "You're not going anywhere until after next week and I don't want you to make him mad until after then either. Next Friday is my Star Day and he might actually show up if you guys don't mess this up!" she bossed.

"Alex," Lauren spoke softly, trying to soothe her daughter, "Honey, we aren't –"

"No Mama, please. Promise me you won't say anything to Uncle Trey until after my Star week. If he's going to be mad at all of us again, I want him to come to my school first."

Lauren and Callie looked at each other trying to figure out a way around this.

"Please, Mama. Daddy can't be there and I need Uncle Trey to be there." Tears streamed down the little girl's cheeks.

Callie reached back and held the little girl's hand in hers. "We won't say anything. We promise."

"And you won't leave?"

"I will stay until after your Star Day, okay? Now wipe your tears."

"Okay," the little girl said between sniffles as she tried to calm herself.

———

TREY SHOWED up right on time and for some reason, it kind of pissed Callie off.

She had paced around the guesthouse for the last forty-five minutes trying to figure out how she was going to spend the next week here without getting any closer to the O'Brien family. She'd promised Alex she'd wait to tell Trey the truth and she intended to keep her promise, but it wasn't going to be easy.

She rubbed her temples, trying to rid some of the tension that had built behind her eyes. Her stomach did the funny flip-flop thing it had been doing since Lauren dropped her off.

She met Trey at the screen door, opening it for him.

"Wow, you look amazing," she said in a breathy whisper, embarrassed by how much his presence affected her. It was just her luck to fall in love with a man who looked like a movie star but could never be hers. She shut the door a little harder behind him than she'd intended.

He looked back at the door first and then slowly at her. "Um, I think that's my line," he drawled, smiling and handing her another daisy.

She couldn't stop the smile that spread across her lips. He really did have a beautiful soul. Another thing that pissed her off for some reason. She thanked him as she walked around the kitchen island and added it to the vase that held the other flowers.

Trey's eyes followed her. "Callie, you are so beautiful. I don't think I've ever told you how truly stunning you are."

Callie blushed, looking down at her retro Guns and Roses t-shirt, skinny jeans, and ballet flats. "Thank you," she snapped. "But you don't have to say things like that."

With furrowed brows, Trey asked, "Why do compliments upset you?"

"It's just..." she blew out an exasperated breath. Little did he know she hung on every word he spoke. Every time his eyes roamed over her face, her body, she felt like the most desired woman in the world.

"Come on, you must have had boys all over you in high school."

Callie released a frustrated laugh. "Our high school experiences were very different."

"Okay... still, are you going to tell me there has never been a person in your life who gave you compliments?"

"It's complicated."

"No, it's really not. I see you, I can clearly see that you are a beautiful, amazingly sexy woman. I tell you so. Couldn't be any easier."

"You can be such an asshole."

His back stiffened and he looked confused. "Why does that make me an asshole?"

"It just does. You continue to refuse to have an open mind to anything. It's okay for someone to have a different life than you, different experiences than you, you know that, right? People don't always have a choice in what happens to them. Sometimes you need to just roll with what life throws at you."

"Whoa, this is taking a strange turn."

"I know, I just... I just don't..." Callie turned her back to him.

"What? You don't what? Tell me."

"I don't know how to respond to compliments, okay? The nicest things people ever said to me when I was growing up were, Hey Callie, your labs look good today, and looks like you've been following your medication schedule as planned. I didn't have a lot of exposure to people who gave me compliments. My mom and dad sure, my sister more so now since we've gotten older, but those always felt so heavy with other things, ya know?"

"No, I don't know," he answered as he gathered her hands in his and led her to the couch.

"Like when my mom would walk in my room and say, Callie, your coloring is so good today. You're such a pretty girl. You know what I heard? Hey Callie, I don't think you're going to die today."

"Jesus, Cal." He reached for her, but she shied away.

"I don't know how to do all of this," she admitted.

"All of what, baby?"

"All of you, and your family, and your crazy number of friends that you've known since you were in utero. I don't know who I'm supposed to be for them." She paused as she looked away, "Or for you."

He reached for her, hooking a finger under her chin and turning her face toward him. "Callie, you crazy girl. You don't have to be anything for me."

"But I do. You just don't know."

"Well how about this? How about we skip the street dance if it's too much for you?"

Callie shook her head.

"Just hear me out. We skip the street dance, go over to Mom's house, and eat some of those delicious leftovers I know she has in her fridge, and then we go to the fireworks."

"But your friends... They're so excited to have you back."

"My friends will understand, believe me. They've known me a long time and ditching them to spend time with a beautiful woman is the most Trey thing I could do."

NINETEEN

Trey pulled off to the side of the gravel road just outside of town and Callie cast him a suspicious look.

"Fireworks start in about twenty minutes. Shouldn't we get into town so we can find somewhere to sit?"

"We already have a front row seat," he said, winking at her as he pulled into a field drive.

"Where are you taking me?"

"Here," he said, a smile crossing his face as he handed her a handkerchief.

"What exactly do you want me to do with this?"

"Blindfold yourself."

"You're joking, right?"

"Could you just trust me for once please?" He batted his eyelashes obnoxiously.

"Okay, fine. If you agree to never do that again," she pleaded as he covered her eyes and tied the cloth behind her head.

Callie held on as the truck bounced and jumped around, finally coming to a stop.

"Now, do you think you can follow directions for once in your life and stay put until I come and get you?"

"You mean you're leaving me in here?" She could feel her anxieties rising.

"I'll be right back. It'll only take me a minute...please, don't look."

"Okay," she agreed as a smile crossed her face.

"Damn, you're beautiful," Trey whispered as he gently caressed her cheek with the tips of his fingers. She leaned toward his touch, suddenly wanting so much more from him.

She sat quietly, her other senses on high alert. She heard the rustling of the grasses outside of the truck and every step that Trey made. The bare skin of her legs rubbed against the seat, making her feel anxious.

"Are you ready?" he asked as he opened her door.

She smiled and nodded her head as he slipped his arm around her shoulders, helping her from the truck. He led her several steps and she giggled as the short grasses tickled her ankles. "What are you up to?"

He slid his hands around her waist from behind and she leaned against his hard chest. His breath tickled her ear as he leaned in, releasing the cloth around her eyes and kissing the shell of her ear.

A shiver escaped as she gasped, covering her mouth with one of her hands. The sun was setting behind the grove of trees that encased their private area, casting shadows over Trey's face. A small fire burned in the middle of a circle of rocks that had been cleared for just that reason. Soft music played from somewhere as the fire crackled.

"Do you like it, Crazy Girl?" he asked as he stepped out from behind her.

She moved toward the fire. "You did this...for me?"

Trey looked at the ground, a shy smile crossing his lips. "I wanted you to have a special memory."

"Oh my god, Trey. Thank you."

"You're welcome."

She reached out and took both of his hands in hers. "No, I mean it. No one has ever done anything like this for me."

Rubbing small circles on the top of her hands with his thumbs, he whispered, "I'm glad it could be me."

He placed a hand at the small of her back, leading her over to the pillows and blankets. She lowered herself to the ground, then he handed her a beer.

"Lauren said it was like looking at the old Trey today."

"Is that bad?" he asked as he laid down on his side facing her, his head propped up on one hand.

She twisted the beer bottle in her hand, "No, not at all, it's just...it's a big change. I have to ask, what happened?"

"What kind of sick were you?" he blurted out.

"Excuse me?" she questioned, unsure what he was asking.

"I want to know, what kind of sick were you?" The flames danced across his face and she watched his beautiful eyes plead with her for honesty. And right then and there, she decided she wasn't going to fight this anymore. The universe was giving her a chance to experience something she never had. She would give Trey as much as she could.

"I was born with a congenital heart defect."

"That sounds serious."

"It was."

"Did you almost die?"

"Yes."

"How many times?"

"What?"

"How many times, Callie? I'm not trying to be insensitive, I really want to know. How many times?"

"Once. Right before my –" Her eyes dropped to the brightly colored quilt she sat on. "Right before my surgery."

He reached for her hand and she happily gave it to him, allowing the touch of his skin on hers to comfort her. He brought her hand to his mouth, kissing her knuckles lightly.

"Is your life anything like it was before? Are you anything like you were before you almost died?"

"No. Everything changed for me that day."

"I died the day Jamie was murdered. Everything inside of me shut down."

Callie took his beer from him and set both of their bottles on top of the cooler. She scooted toward him until her knees were touching his chest. He traced a finger along her knee and up her thigh, leaving goose bumps where his touch had been.

"I'm not the same person," he continued. "I never will be. Like you, everything changed for me."

She ran her fingers up his arm that now was draped over her knee. "I think it's okay to be changed. I would be more worried if you told me your brother's death didn't change you."

"I don't know how to get back to who I used to be. I'm lost."

"I think you're just starting over, and it scares you. If there is one thing my illness taught me, it's okay to be afraid."

"What scares you?"

Callie pulled a pillow over, laying her head down as he moved in closer so they were both facing each other. She ran her fingers down the side of his face, "Never feeling like this again."

"When I met you, you made me want to feel again. And I couldn't, I didn't even know how. I'd been shut down for so long and been at such a distance from everyone and everything, I'd forgotten what it was like to just breathe."

"Coming back to the farm made you feel that. Seeing your mom gardening again made you feel that. Being around Lauren and Alex made you –"

He quickly cupped the back of her head and pulled her to him, nose to nose, "Kissing you made me feel it all."

A soft whimper escaped her as his lips came down on hers. They were soft at first, unraveling every rigid and closed-off part of her soul. Her heart overflowed with emotion, beating with a new type of energy as his kisses grew hungry. She opened for him and as their tongues met, she moaned into his mouth. And suddenly his hands were gently fisting her hair, moving her exactly where he needed her to be. His touch awakening a submissive need in her until he broke their kiss.

She moaned as she threw her leg over and straddled him, taking her turn to claim him with her mouth. She paused long enough to pull her t-shirt over her head. He brushed her hair away from her face, and she lowered herself back down, their rapid breaths tangling in between them.

"Are you sure?" he asked, his voice low and raspy.

She kissed him again, this time pouring all the confusion and hurt, mixed with the trust and hope that their entire journey promised, however long it lasted. "Yes. Please," she panted as he slowly rolled her onto her back. Her hand went to the back of his neck, pulling him to her again.

He trailed his nose lightly along her jaw. She inhaled deeply, arching her back as he moved down her neck. Her breath caught in her throat as he lowered his mouth to her scar. Small tears escaped as he placed a lingering kiss where her scar began and continued to press tender kisses until he reached the end.

Every little touch, every breath, every heartbeat of his called to her without regret. She knew she needed this man more than she remembered needing anything else.

"I know I can't heal every hurt you've ever had, but I think I'm ready to start over, and maybe we can heal each other along the way. How does that sound?"

"I think it sounds like a beautiful love story."

His hands slowly moved down her bare stomach, his fingers found the snap on her jeans. "Our love story."

Sensing her body tensing, he pulled back slightly. "I haven't... I've never done this before," she admitted, her eyes looking into his, needing understanding and permission to be who she was in this moment – scared, but willing to give into him completely.

He rested his forehead against hers. "Don't worry, I've got you," he whispered softly.

She smiled as she pulled him in, "And I've got you."

TWENTY

THE MORNING SUN PEEKED THROUGH THE WINDOWS, warming Callie's face. She inhaled deeply and was filled with a type of peace she'd never known and knew it was because she was sore in all the right ways and all the right places. Trey shifted next to her and wrapped his big arm around her waist, pulling her close, her back to his front. She snuggled herself against him and he growled his appreciation.

"'Good Morning," his gravelly voice whispered as he buried his face in her hair. "I think we should call in sick and stay in bed all day."

Callie giggled and pulled his arm even more tightly around herself. "I should call in sick to who? Your Mom?"

Trey propped himself up on one elbow, enjoying the smile he knew he was responsible for. Pressing his hard chest against her back, he leaned down and kissed her neck. "Yes, I'm sure –"

"Callie? Callie Loftier, are you here?" The new voice floated up from the first floor.

Callie gasped and pulled Trey down on top of her, trying

to see over his shoulder. She covered his mouth with both hands as her eyes anxiously searched the stairway like she expected someone to be standing there. "Didn't you lock the door?" she whisper-yelled, as panic washed across her face.

"Who is it?" Trey mumbled from behind her fingers. She shook her head frantically, pleading with him to be quiet and let her handle it.

"Callie? Is that you?"

Callie slid out from under Trey. "Yep, I'll be right down," she hollered as she rolled off the bed, scrambling to gather her clothes from the floor.

"Callie," Trey said in a poor attempt at a whisper, "who the hell is down there?"

"Oh my god, you were right. This place is amazing!"

"Yep...uh huh," Callie called out as she continued the search for her clothes. Trey rolled off the other side of the bed and popped his head up to look at her. Callie threw his shorts at him, landing them in his face. She pointed at his other clothes in a silent command for him to get dressed.

But instead, Trey crawled over to the edge of the loft. He needed to get a peek at the person who had Callie all riled up. She grabbed him by the ankle, pulling on his leg to stop him. "No, please" she begged.

"Who's down there?" he asked again as he looked back at her.

"Trey...please...can you stay up here and be quiet until I figure out what I'm going to do?"

"You want me to hide?"

"No...just don't be seen."

Trey sat up quickly and pulled her on top of him, his arms trapping her, holding her tightly as she tried to escape. "Isn't that the definition of hiding?"

Callie squirmed and pushed against his chest. "Tell me who is down there."

"Please, Trey."

He kissed her quickly while grabbing her ass with both hands, "Tell me...or I'll go dancing down those steps in all my glory and introduce myself."

"No, no, no. Please." Anxiety was suddenly rolling off her in waves, making him feel bad for teasing her and even making his stomach drop a little. Whoever it was, Callie was concerned. He loosened his grip just as the stairs made a creaking sound.

"Well, well, well. I guess plans have changed a bit since the last time we talked." Jade Loftier stood at the top of the stairs. Her dark skinny jeans complemented her small frame just as perfectly as her red, fitted top complemented her fiery personality. A string of classic pearls adorned her neck and was her go-to look. Her hair was a warmer shade of blonde than Callie's honey-colored locks. But it was her dark brown eyes that Callie had always been so in awe of. They were steadfast and warm, and Callie has trusted those eyes to tell her the truth in even her darkest times. But right now, she could feel those eyes burning into her. She dropped her head, dramatically sighing. Speaking into Trey's chest because she didn't want to make eye contact with either of them, she waved a hand in her sister's direction, "Trey O'Brien, I'd like to introduce you to Jade Loftier, my sister."

"Oh shit," Trey mumbled and dropped the back of his head to the floor.

Jade cleared her throat, clearly enjoying this. "I can see the two of you may need a moment," she said with a smirk. "I'll wait for you downstairs."

Callie waited only a few seconds before pushing herself off Trey's chest and giving it a playful slap.

"That went well, don't you think?" Trey asked as he jumped up and pulled on his shorts.

Callie just shook her head and laughed, "Shut up, Trey."

"What? I think she liked me," he grinned as he pulled on his t-shirt and sauntered over to Callie. She wrapped her arms around his waist and pulled him close. "I'm so embarrassed."

"Why? We're two adults doing the things two adults do, Crazy Girl. And we do it well." He smiled and slapped her ass as he released her and picked up her shirt from the floor and handed it to her. "Besides, it's good I get to meet some of your family. You know all of mine, so it's only fair."

"But I didn't want it to be like this. My sister and I are close, and I wanted the chance to explain things before she knew we were together."

Callie stilled, her shirt halfway on. Trey grasped the bottom of her shirt and slowly helped her pull it down over her head. When her shirt was in place, she noticed he was looking directly into her eyes. "Is that what this is, Cal? Are we together?" Trey asked as he pointed back and forth between the two of them.

Callie wanted to look away as she felt the blush spreading to her cheeks, but she couldn't. There was something in his eyes, a softness that made her long to hold him in her arms and forget all the reasons why this shouldn't be happening.

"I mean...I guess we –" She stammered and glanced back at the bed.

Trey gently held her chin, turning her face to his, "Baby, if that's your way of asking me where I am in all of this?

Then yes. I'm here and not going anywhere. I can be kind of a handful, Miss Loftier. Are you up for the challenge?"

Callie smiled and nodded her head, knowing everything about this was wrong, but she just couldn't fight it any longer.

"Okay then," he said as he dropped a quick kiss on her forehead, "let's go meet the sister...with clothes on this time."

Callie turned toward the steps but Trey grabbed her hand. She turned to face him, expecting more teasing but instead there was something else. "Cal, I want you to know..." he paused, running his thumb over the top of her hand. "I'm not good at this. Words. Feelings."

Broken people share themselves in different ways. For others, it would seem like a small gesture, but for someone like Trey, it was monumental. She felt his hand tremble. Instinctively, she covered it with her other hand. A smile lifted the edge of his lips as he looked at their joined hands.

"Thank you," he said, his words rushing out. "You were so unexpected, and I guess I needed that."

"I've spent the last two years, wishing I could go back to the worst moment of my life. When regret and fear fill your every thought, a future for yourself becomes an unnecessary thing... an unwanted thing. You don't make plans, you don't think of the next times. It's nothing more than an unbearable extension of the painful reality you've created. I don't think anyone else in my life would understand that, but I think you do."

Callie's eyes filled with tears as she reached up and lightly touched his cheek. "I do," she said.

"I'm an asshole and a moody SOB, but I promise, if you're willing to stick around, I promise to try as hard as I can to make a life without my brother. I don't know what that looks like, or where to even start, but I hope you'll be by my side while I try to figure it out."

A tear rolled down her cheek as she smiled up at him. Trey's eyebrows pulled together, his lips turning down slightly. "A smile and a tear? Are you happy or sad?"

"I'm both. I'm sad that both of us have had to face such deep hurts and fears in our lives. But I'm so happy that circumstances have brought us together to help us heal. And I'm hopeful this really is the beginning for us and we can move forward together, regardless of the past."

Trey pulled her to him, whispering into her hair as she hugged him back. "A new beginning?"

"Our new beginning," Callie said confidently.

"That's right," he agreed as he leaned into her lips and whispered, "our new beginning."

Trey climbed down the steps, Callie just one step behind and gripping his hand tightly.

Jade watched them from her stool at the kitchen island. "Jesus, you two make quite the dramatically beautiful entrance."

Trey walked over to her, a hand extended. "Jade, I'm sorry to have met you like that. Callie is embarrassed and I take all the blame for what you saw upstairs. I'm Trey. Welcome to the O'Brien farm."

Jade took Trey's hand and stood. "Thank you, Trey. I appreciate that but," she pointed up toward the loft, "it didn't look like my sister was being forced to do anything she didn't want to do, was she?"

"Nope."

"Then I would only take half the blame if I were you." She smiled brightly at him.

Callie rushed past Trey and embraced her sister. Trey

watched the way she melted into Jade. Her sister was home, she was safe.

"I'm so glad you're here, but why didn't you tell me you were coming?"

"Because you would've told me not to come because you were fine and there was nothing to worry about."

Trey blew out an exaggerated breath and both girls looked at him. He put his hands up in front of himself in surrender. "What? She knows you well, doesn't she?" He grabbed two coffee cups and held them up toward the sisters.

"Yes, please." They said in unison. Trey's eyes widened in surprise as he laughed at their enthusiastic reaction to the prospect of coffee.

Callie turned back to Jade. "But I really am fine, and there isn't anything to worry about."

Jade's eyes glanced quickly to Trey and then back to Callie. "I think we need to talk a little bit about that."

"About what?"

"About if you really are doing fine."

Callie nodded her head slowly, hoping her sister would see how much she cared for Trey. "Yes, I really am." Callie knew exactly what her sister was asking, but this was not happening now. Especially after everything Trey had just said to her upstairs. She knew she was in love with him, and no one was going to take that from her. Not even Jade.

"So, you'll be coming home soon? That's always been the plan, right?"

"I'm not sure yet," Callie said quietly, letting her eyes fall to the floor.

"Callie?" Trey questioned, his voice concerned as he set the cups down.

Jade continued like Trey wasn't even in the room. "Do you have your next destination in mind?"

"No, not yet."

"Callie...tell her. Tell her what our plan is." Trey encouraged as he came to stand next to them.

Jade looked up from her sister, tipping her head to the side and settling her eyes on Trey. "I'm trying to decide if my sister is safe here with you. There are many things about Callie I'm sure you don't know about."

Trey released a tight laugh and slid his arm around Callie's waist. "She'll always be safe when she's with me."

"Is that right?" Jade asked, her eyes tightening around the edges as she took a step back and crossed her arms over her chest.

"Yes, that's right."

Jade pursed her lips, lifting one eyebrow. "I've been taking care of her all of her life. You have sex with her one time and suddenly you think you know everything about her?"

"First of all," Trey pointed out as he moved his arm up and draped it over Callie's shoulders, "it was more than one time."

"Trey," Callie said, embarrassed, as she rubbed her forehead.

"Okay, sorry, probably inappropriate, but no. I don't think I know everything about her because a woman like Callie is a constant surprise. She surprises me every day with her strength and her stubbornness. She's silly sometimes and sassy the next, and I never really know what to expect. But if there is one thing I do know, she can take care of herself. She doesn't need me or you to do that for her. She will always be safe with me because I will protect her heart and who she is because she deserves that. But as far as taking care of her...she does a fine job of that on her own."

Jade smiled at Trey, and then at her sister and shook her head. "Well, you were right about one thing – he's a charmer." Both girls laughed, breaking the tension in the room.

"Umm, thanks?" Trey said as he looked back and forth between the sisters, completely confused about what was happening.

"I think I need to talk to my sister alone," Callie said as she gently turned him around and started walking him toward the door.

"Of course." Trey leaned down to gently kiss her on the cheek, "I'll be at the main house." He looked to Jade. "Are we good?"

She gave him two thumbs up, "We sure are, cowboy."

"Okay," he said doubtfully, drawing out the word like he didn't exactly trust her words. "I'll let my mom know you'll be joining us for dinner."

Jade nodded her head, "Okay, see you later."

As soon as Trey left, Callie walked around the couch, letting herself flop onto the comfortable cushions. "I don't want to sound like I'm not excited to see you, but seriously, what are you doing here?"

"Callie...I'm worried about you."

Callie's head dropped against the back of the couch. "Why?"

Jade's mouth fell open, then she pointed from the bedroom to Callie, to the screen door where Trey had just left. "Oh, I don't know. Do I need to recap for you? This boy could really hurt you." She fell onto the couch next to her sister, letting her head fall back, copying Callie. They sat in silence, staring at the ceiling until Jade finally spoke again barely above a whisper, "What are you doing, Cal?"

"I don't know, but I think I'm in love with him. Like...for the first time in my life, I truly care about someone."

Jade picked up Callie's hand, pulling it into her lap. "And it's pretty obvious he cares about you. Does he know yet?"

"No." Callie rested her head on her sister's shoulder as tears rolled down her face. Jade patted her sister's cheek like she used to do when Callie was little and not feeling well, laying her head on top of hers.

"Holy shit," Jade groaned, taking a deep breath, "you're going to ruin him."

Callie snuggled into the comfort of her sister and let her heart break for all the secrets she'd been forced to keep. None of this was her fault, but she continued to selfishly hold onto Trey even when everything except her heart told her to let him go. She'd come here with the hopes of being the one to bring him peace and put the entire family back together. But it was becoming a real possibility that she might be the one to deliver the final blow for all of them.

"Oh, Cal," Jade said sympathetically. "I wasn't kidding when I said the two of you made a dramatically beautiful entrance, but I'm afraid it's going to be a tragically explosive exit. And to be honest, I'm not sure either of you will make it out in one piece."

TWENTY-ONE

"Callie, relax. Let's just have a nice dinner." Jade said as she and Callie crossed the yard toward the main house. "But I do think some serious conversations need to happen between his family and us. They must understand how devastating this could be for both of you. They need to prepare for what might happen."

"Or might not, maybe it'll all work out. No one wants the truth out more than me. But Alex's Star Day is this Friday and I promised her, and I won't let her down."

Jade stopped walking, "Seriously? The seven-year-old niece? You can't let her down?"

"You'll understand once you meet her."

As if on cue, Trey came out onto the porch holding Alex's hand. "There she is, Firefly."

"Callie," she squealed as she skipped down the stairs and launched herself at Callie. "Guess what? Last night at the lock-in..." she stopped mid-thought and tipped her head and turned toward Jade. "Those are some kick-butt pearls. Where did you get them?"

"Um..." Jade looked at Callie for a second and then back

down to Alex. "Honestly, I bought them from a street vendor in New York City."

"Rad. Are they stolen?"

Trey threw his head back and barked out a laugh, "Why in the world would you ask her that? What do you know about stolen jewelry."

Alex rolled her eyes at Trey's reaction, "It's just a question. I watched a show on Netflix about New York and the mob's underground activities. There's some shady stuff going on in that town if you know what I mean." She looked back at Jade with squinted eyes, "And by the looks of those pearls, I think you do." She winked, her entire face lighting up with the famous O'Brien smile.

Trey turned toward the screen door and yelled, "Lauren! Are you letting my niece watch Netflix? Seriously? And now she knows about mob activity in New York? Am I the only one that understands she is only seven?"

"Alex, it's time to eat...and Trey, you need to relax," Lauren called from inside the kitchen.

"Be right there," Alex responded as she started walking backward toward the steps. "You should totally tell people you bought them from the mob. Way cooler story." She gave two thumbs up, then spun around and ran up the steps and disappeared into the house.

Jade's mouth hung open slightly as she stared toward the house. A little breath escaped from her as she pointed to the empty porch, speechless. Callie nodded her head with a smirk on her face, watching as Jade absorbed all that was Alexandria O'Brien.

"I totally get it," Jade said in understanding as she followed behind Callie. "I think I want to be that kid's best friend."

The formal dining room was set up with candles, cloth

napkins, and formal settings. "I hope you didn't go to all this fuss for me, Mrs. O'Brien," Jade said as she followed Callie into the room.

"They did," Alex chirped as she snagged a black olive from the relish tray.

"Hush, Alex," Eve scolded as she waved a hand in her direction. "This is fun for me, so thank you for giving me a reason to fuss a little bit. And please, sweetheart, call me Eve." She insisted and pulled Jade into a tight embrace. "So nice to meet you."

"And I've heard you've already met my son, Trey. I apologize for that."

"Hey," Trey grumbled, a celery stick hanging from his mouth and one arm already draped over Callie's shoulder. Alex and Callie giggled at him.

"And my granddaughter, Alex," she nodded toward the girl, "who is really just a smaller version of her Uncle Trey."

Trey and Alex exchanged grins and nodded their heads in agreement, giving each other a fist bump.

"This is her mama, Lauren, and her boyfriend, Andy. Andy manages the farm for us and has been one of Trey's best friends since they were little."

"I don't even like him," Trey said and punched Andy in the arm.

"Quit playing, Uncle Trey. We all know you and Andy are homies."

"Whaa... homies?" Trey asked, a horrified expression on his face.

"It means friends," she informed him as she walked around the table to her regular spot.

"I know what it –" Trey looked at his sister-in-law, "Lauren?"

"Alex, can you please stop picking on your uncle? Can't you see you've got him all worked up?"

Alex giggled and pulled out the chair next to her. "Jade, you can sit by me if you want.

"I sure do," she said excitedly as she rounded the table. "Thank you so much for having me, Eve. I know this was short notice, so I really appreciate the hospitality."

Trey slid his hand to the small of Callie's back, pulling out the chair across the table from Jade and whispering in her ear, "You're going to sit next to me, beautiful." He took the seat at the end of the table but continued to hold Callie's hand as everyone took their seats.

"Not a problem at all, dear. Let's eat, shall we?"

The conversation continued comfortably throughout the meal. Jade shared stories of Callie as a child, being careful not to mention her illness. Andy told stories of what it was like to grow up as a third wheel with the O'Brien boys.

Alex talked about Star Day and what would happen. She told everyone where they should sit and invited Jade to come too.

Although Jade could totally see why her sister had fallen in love with this family, it didn't change the fact this was a dangerous situation. She watched out of the corner of her eye as Callie and Trey held their own secret conversations. A touch here, a look there...smiles meant only for each other.

After dessert, Alex left the table to go watch cartoons and the mood in the room took a different turn.

Jade cleared her throat. "I want to thank you for such a lovely night, Eve, but I think it's only fair that I bring up the elephant in the room."

"Jade, please." Callie pleaded as she set down her glass.

Trey reached for Callie's hand and held it tightly. A united front.

"Jade, I know you're concerned, but I really think this is between Callie and me. I don't understand why you're so worried about your sister. She is a grown woman. Have I done something to make you think I'm an asshole or I'm going to hurt her?"

Jade turned toward Trey, her eyes first falling to their joined hands, and then back to Callie's pleading eyes. "Trey, it's not that I think you're a bad person at all. In fact, you have as much to lose as my sister. I'm as concerned about you as I am her." Jade addressed the whole room. "I know I'm not the only one here who can see that these two are falling hard for each other."

Callie shook her head, tears threatening to fall as she looked at her sister. "I can't do this, I won't give him up," she said with conviction as she pushed herself away from the table.

"Callie, what the hell are you talking about? Nobody is giving anyone up." Trey's voice was getting louder.

"Please, I'm not trying to upset any of you. I just want you..." she looked at each face around the table, "I want all of you to look at this through clearer eyes. I don't know how much you all know about..." Jade paused, and her eyes shot to Callie, "my sister's illness. But I can't allow her to set herself up for something she may not be capable of recovering from."

Jade stood, silently begging her sister, "He says no one is giving up anyone but I've almost lost you too many times to be okay with this."

"Now, girls. Please sit. I'm sure we can work through this without anyone getting hurt or upset."

"With all due respect, Eve, I don't think you have my sister's best interest in mind."

"I love Callie. She has gotten me through some tough times," Eve said gently.

"I know exactly what Callie has done for you and believe me, I know exactly what your family has done for Callie, and I do not have the words to thank you for that. But in all honesty, in this situation, all you can see is this," Jade pointed at Trey standing, holding onto Callie with a confused look on his face. "All you know is right now, at this moment, he is here. He is part of your family again and you don't want anything to jeopardize that."

Eve's eyes filled with tears before she covered her face with both hands.

"I, on the other hand, can see both sides of this. When she loses him, she also loses all of you plus that adorable little girl in the other room. Where does that leave her?"

Trey pounded his fist on the table, "Stop right there. Who said anything about me leaving Callie? Why are you so sure that's going to happen?"

Jade pointed across the table at him, "You don't understand what's at risk here. I see her with you. I see her in a way I've never seen her before. She's alive. Finally, she is fully alive." She turned toward Andy and Lauren who was wiping tears from her eyes. "I see her like you see Trey. But we all know this is dangerous."

"What the hell are you talking about? Callie, I'm sorry I called you crazy. Obviously, your sister has that title in your family."

"I didn't come here to stop this, I came here to offer support to my sister. I came here because when I talked to her yesterday, I could hear the struggle in her voice. She cares about you, Trey. Deeply. I don't know about the rest of you, but I can feel it in the room right now. The two of you together are magnetic."

"And why is that a bad thing?"

Jade paused. "Because...it is," she said, her voice full of empathy.

"Damn it! Will someone please tell me what the hell is going on?" He looked from person to person, each of them struggling with what to say. "I've finally just started living again, and you're going to waltz in here and tell me that's wrong? I haven't wanted to feel anything since my brother died, and Callie is the first real thing in my life. She's funny and beautiful and perfect for me. So, will someone please explain to me why us being together is such a horrible idea."

Jade kept her eyes on Callie, waiting for the truth to come out. Promise to Alex or not, Trey deserved to know. And even if this wasn't the plan for tonight, after watching the two of them together, it was so clear to Jade that this couldn't go on any longer.

Trey slammed his fist on the table again, this time hard enough to make the water slosh around in the glasses. Callie jumped as tears streamed down her face, "Someone tell me what is going on!"

Callie opened her mouth and Jade held her breath. "I tried to kill myself," she blurted.

The room went silent.

"Callie, no..." Jade whispered, and she let her body fall back into her chair.

The words came out in a rush. "Right before my... surgery. I was so sick and weak, and I felt like such a burden on Jade and my parents. I convinced myself they would be better off without me. I couldn't take it anymore, so I tried to kill myself."

Jade covered her mouth with one hand and looked away from the table. She couldn't watch this anymore.

"My sister is afraid if things don't work out between the two of us, I won't be able to recover and I might try again."

Eve stood, rushed around the table and wrapped her arms around Callie, "Oh honey, you will never lose us like that. Yes, it's true that any relationship is a risk. But it's worth it, don't you think?"

She reached up and smoothed one side of Callie's hair. "You are fortunate you have a sister who cares so much about you, that she would come all the way here to make sure you're okay."

"I already know about the suicide attempt," Trey confessed.

"What?" Eve's eyes widened as she looked at her son. "How could you possibly know that?"

"Callie knows this but, I've had Sheriff Deal looking into her background."

"Trey, honey. You didn't." Eve pulled out a chair from the table and Callie helped her sit down.

"Mama, she shows up here out of the blue and suddenly everything changes. I didn't know a thing about her and I wasn't sure if you did either."

"But having the Sheriff poking around in her background?"

"I know, it was stupid, but that's how I found out her last name. He also knew she had a chronic illness of some type and that she had attempted suicide. That's when it all fell into place."

"What did?" Lauren asked. "What fell into place?"

"Mom had told me about a group she found online where you could share your feelings with other people who had been sick or lost loved ones. She had mentioned that she had met some amazing people who were helping her get through her grief. I asked Callie about it and she said yes, that's where they met."

The room was silent as Trey's gaze circled the table and stopped on Callie, who was standing next to him. He reached for her hands. "Callie, do you have any idea what you've done in the short time you've been here?"

Callie's tears streamed down her face.

"You've got my mom planting flowers, hosting events, having BBQ's. Do you know how big that is? Because of you, I'm in the process of accepting the fact that this big dummy right here might actually be able to take care of Lauren and Firefly."

"And..." he placed his hand over his chest, "I feel this beating again. Really beating, not only to keep me alive but because I want to have a life. That's what you've done for me, you've given me my life back."

He wrapped his arm around Callie's waist and she leaned into him. "We're leaving. Mom, could you please fix one of the bedrooms up for Jade tonight?"

"Of course."

Trey looked down at Jade. "We can talk more about this tomorrow but right now, I need to take Callie home. I hope you understand."

Jade didn't look at him, she just nodded her head a couple times and whispered, "Home," her eyes dropping to her lap.

After Callie and Trey left, Jade looked up to find Andy comforting Lauren.

"Well, that didn't go exactly as planned, did it?"

"Jade, I'm so sorry I had you come all this way and got you involved in this." Eve apologized, "I just can't figure a way out of this. I knew the feelings they had for each other were strong, but this? I fear I've made more mistakes than can be counted."

"I can't believe she would use her suicide attempt as an aversion to the real story. She must be terrified of losing him." Jade tried to swallow past the lump in her throat. "I don't see this ending in any other way but heartache."

Jade looked at the couple sitting across the table. "And I'm pretty sure this train wreck is going to end with us losing them both."

TWENTY-TWO

It had been several days and no one had spoken about the disaster of a dinner that had happened the first night Jade arrived. She'd come to the conclusion they were great people and great at loving each other, but also great at avoiding the situation in front of them.

"Are you sure you want to go out tonight? I mean, seriously, who goes out for drinks on a Thursday night?" Jade asked her sister as she pulled off her gardening gloves and threw them onto the island. "You've been with him every night since I got here."

"Is baby Jade pouting?" Callie teased in a child-like voice, tilting her head to the side. She laughed as Jade stuck out her bottom lip and dramatically stomped her foot, faking a tantrum.

She wrapped her arms around Jade, pinning her arms to her body and squeezed her tightly. "You might even have some fun." Callie gave her sister a quick peck on the cheek, then released her and headed toward the kitchen to make some lunch. "And lots of people go out for drinks on Thursday night. You live in New York, for goodness sake.

Don't tell me you leave work every night and head straight home to get your beauty rest."

"I know, but this is different. This town has one bar." Jade held up one finger and shook it in the air. "One bar, Cal."

"So? What's your point? That just means everyone will be in the same place."

"That. That's my point, right there. Even if every person who lives in this town goes, it will still be..." Jade searched for the right word, "boring." She drew out the word like she might actually die from lack of entertainment. She flopped onto the couch and threw an arm over her eyes.

Callie laughed as she opened the refrigerator and leaned in to grab the left-over sloppy joe meat she'd brought home from Eve's the night before.

Jade propped up on her elbows. "Hey, I could stay here and watch Alex. At least that kid is cool. We could watch some of those Netflix shows she's been telling me about."

"Nope. Sorry, but you're going. You know, you might actually like it here if you give it a try." Callie turned toward the microwave to warm up the loose meat.

Jade took a long, deep breath. She couldn't deny there was something about the sweet solitude of the farm that called to her. At night, when she and Callie would sit out on the back porch with nothing but the moon reflecting off the lazy, flowing stream, she understood. It was the kind of calm that seeped into your soul searching out the aching parts with a soft, healing touch. She'd never found anything like this in the city.

Even the beach house didn't offer this kind of peace. Although, she suspected the memories it held had something to do with that. Their mom had always tried to make that place bright and cheerful, bringing in fresh flowers and always changing up the décor to keep it new. Fresh. But everyone knew it was the 'waiting place.' They were either waiting for Callie to get the lifesaving call or waiting for her to die.

She was tired and sore. Eve had worked them hard the last few days getting ready for the upcoming event the O'Brien's were hosting. Although she had never planted a thing in her life, she'd been Callie's assistant and really enjoyed being outside in the fresh air.

Her sister stood at the island, humming a tune while setting out the food, and suddenly Jade's heart constricted tightly in her chest. Her sister was...happy She was as healthy as she had ever been and there was something else. She was in love.

Not the juvenile kind of stuff they'd sat on Callie's bed and dreamed about as young girls. It was so apparent to Jade now. This was real, deep love that people look for every day.

The kind that makes a person whole.

The kind that is both your greatest strength and your greatest weakness. A connection to another human being that stretches who you are as a person and allows you to become more than you ever believed you were capable of.

But it was also the type that took everything with it when it was gone. It ground out the last bit of who you were when you had it and destroyed the future you'd planned when it left. The absence of it raged like a fiery demon consuming your spirit and changing the direction of your path.

But Callie was too far in now and her sister knew it. There was no stopping it. All she could do was be here for the fallout.

Jade sat down across from her sister and gave her a forced smile. "Tomorrow's the day. Are you ready?"

Callie continued to busy herself with retrieving containers of leftovers and spooning them into dishes. She kept her back to her sister, "Yep, I'm ready." Jade couldn't help but notice the sudden acceleration of Callie's breathing.

Callie spun around, the bowl of macaroni salad shaking in her hand as she tried to set it down. Jade rushed around the island and took it from her and set it on the counter.

"Cal?" She asked with concern, reaching for her sister when she saw her sway, holding onto her upper arms.

Callie trembled in her arms, her face suddenly ashen. Jade pulled her in and held her close, stroking her sister's hair like she used to when they were both young girls and scared Callie was destined to succumb to her illness.

"Shh. Just concentrate on your breathing, Sis. In and out. I'm right here."

Jade's eyes burned with unshed tears as they shared an unspoken understanding.

Callie would lose Trey to the truth that he deserved to know.

"I can't...I can't..." Callie gasped and cried as she took comfort in her sister's embrace.

TWENTY-THREE

Jade slammed the door of Callie's car, stepping onto the sidewalk and smoothing her peach-colored sundress down as she looked around the main street of the town that had crawled its way into her sister's heart. There wasn't much to see – a bank, a craft store, something that looked like a hardware store, and a post office. Down the block sat a brown building which looked more like a warehouse than a bar. If it wasn't for the obnoxious, flashing sign poking out of the front of it with the name Tipsy's scrawled across it in the worst font possible, Jade was sure she would've walked past it, assuming there was nothing but tractors parked inside.

Callie grabbed Jade's hand as they walked up the sidewalk toward the lone bar in town. She'd promised Jade the best-tasting pizza she had ever had, which was a significant promise considering she'd been living in New York City for the last two years. Just thinking about it made her stomach growl loudly.

"You okay?" Callie laughed as Jade put her hand on her stomach.

"No," Jade complained as her sister pulled her along. "I'm sore, exhausted, and starving. Eve is like a pocket-sized Army sergeant. I've never worked so hard in my life."

Callie rolled her eyes, "Okay, drama queen. I think you'll survive."

Callie didn't slow at all, forcing Jade to continue her quick steps. "Oh, and I should warn you," Callie mentioned, glancing over her shoulder. "At this time of night, there will be people in here eating pizza with their kids."

Jade frowned, pulling her eyebrows together as she rushed after her sister. "I thought we were going to a bar?"

"We are."

"So...kids are allowed in bars here? What the hell kind of place is this?" Jade asked with a hint of humor in her voice.

"Well, they serve food, too."

"So, it's a restaurant?"

"Yes, that too."

"This town is so weird," she mumbled under her breath, almost running into her sister who had stopped a few feet short of the front door.

When Callie didn't say anything, Jade stepped up next to her, nudging her sister's shoulder with her own. "How about you? You good?"

Callie took in a deep breath and nodded, forcing a smile as she squeezed her sister's hand. "I don't have a choice anymore, do I?"

Jade slowly shook her head. "No, not really."

"I have to see it through to the end and hope like hell he forgives me."

"He's an idiot if he doesn't." Jade meant every word of it. As scared as she was for her sister if Trey O'Brien couldn't see what a catch Callie was, it was his loss. She wasn't exactly sure she was ready to lose her sister to small hick town, USA, but would take that any day over the broken heart she sensed her sister stood on the edge of.

Callie looked away from Tipsy's and down the empty Main Street. "And if he doesn't?" she wondered, not really a question to Jade but more to herself.

"I don't know," Jade answered honestly. "I guess we deal with whatever happens."

Callie forced out a small smile as she centered herself with a deep breath but still didn't move. Jade grabbed her sister's other hand and pulled them up between them, forcing Callie to turn and look her in the eye.

"Okay?" Jade asked with a touch of encouragement in her voice.

"Okay," Callie responded with something that sounded more like acceptance.

Jade was pleasantly surprised at how full the place was. The booths and tables in the front part were filled with families trying to eat quickly while their kids ran back and forth from their seats to the old-time arcade games lining the opposite wall.

"Hey, guys, over here!" Lauren shouted as she waved at them from the table in the back of the building. Jade followed Callie across a small, empty dance floor. There was a band setting up on the stage to the left and Jade could see the fully stocked bar that ran along the back wall.

She laughed as they approached the table and looked at Lauren, "Why do I feel like I just crossed over to the wrong side of the tracks?"

Lauren smiled and opened her mouth to respond but before she could, a thick, husky voice ran over Jade's skin, making her turn around, facing a giant of a man behind her.

"But doesn't the wrong side feel good?" He held out his hand to her, "I'm Jesse."

"Dear God, aren't you beautiful," Jade admired aloud as he wrapped his calloused hand around hers.

"You're not so bad yourself," he lifted one eyebrow and gave a quick nod of his head in her direction and took a drink of his beer. Jade thought she saw a hint of pink blushing across his cheeks.

"Stop it, Jess," Callie scolded as she playfully slapped at his arm. "This is my sister Jade. Jade, this is everyone," mimicking the way Trey had introduced her to his friends.

Trey adjusted his chair and offered his lap to Callie. "Come here, Crazy Girl. I haven't seen you all day." She sat down, wrapping her arms around his neck as he hugged her close, rubbing softly up and down her back. "I missed you. Where have you been? I thought maybe you changed your mind and skipped town on me."

Callie tensed, her face draining of color.

"Nope, it was my fault," Jade admitted. "I didn't know what to wear to a restaurant slash bar slash arcade slash dance hall." Everyone chuckled except Trey. She knew he didn't trust her and he was smart not to. If she had her way, she would take Callie far away from all of this and protect her from the fallout that would soon happen. She waved her hand in the air, "I must've changed a hundred times."

Jesse pulled out the chair next to Trey and Callie and offered it to Jade. She paused as her stomach did a funny, little flip thing. "Thank you," she said to Jesse and he flashed her a smile and gave her a wink. You chose well because you look beautiful. You both do."

"Thanks, Jesse," Callie said appreciatively.

Trey tightened his grip around Callie's midsection.

"Are you hungry?"

"Famished. I think we finally got all the planting done for the fundraiser."

"Your mom certainly knows how to put a girl to work, Trey. So much for my vacation in the country." Jade crossed her arms over her chest, trying to look upset but couldn't keep a straight face when Lauren started laughing.

"Thanks for showing up, Jade. Otherwise, I would've been the one out there next to your sister."

"I didn't really do much except whatever Callie told me to. She's just as bossy as Eve. But honestly, I don't know if you guys have noticed, but my sister has a real talent with flowers."

"Jade," Callie said, trying to hush her sister.

"No, it's true, Cal," she affirmed, reaching for some shelled peanuts from the bucket in the middle of the table. "You really do. You are so happy when you're doing it."

"I've noticed," Trey chimed in, silencing everyone around him.

"You fit in here, Callie. I hope you know that. This is where you belong, here with me. With all of us." He leaned in and gave her a soft kiss as Jade made eye contact with a worried Lauren. "I hope you're here to stay."

Callie wrapped her arms around his neck, laying her head on his shoulder, tears wetting her eyes.

"Who wants another drink?" Andy blurted, standing abruptly.

"Just get a couple of pitchers and tell them to put it on my tab," Trey instructed, making Andy turn around toward the group.

"Why don't you guys come with me?" he suggested. "Leave the ladies to talk about us behind our backs."

Trey stood and kissed Callie's hand whispering, "I'll be right back."

"Come on, Romeo," Jesse teased as he slapped a hand on his friend's shoulder. "She can't escape. Unless she's smart and bolts out the back door." He smiled and winked at Callie.

Trey gave him a slight shove, "Don't give her any ideas, dumbass."

As soon as they were out of earshot, Lauren leaned in. "Everything is going to be okay." She reached across the table and held Callie's hands.

"She's right," added Jade. "There's nothing to be upset about tonight. Dance with Trey. Let him hold you and whisper all those sweet things to you. You deserve to be happy."

"Even if it's only for tonight?" Callie asked, her eyes dropping to the table.

Lauren let out a long breath, leaning against the back of her chair, "For as long as it lasts."

TWENTY-FOUR

"Jade, are you ready? We can't be late."

Jade hopped down the stairs, trying to get one shoe on her foot while holding the other in her hand. "Have you seen my black and white scarf?"

Callie pointed to the other side of the living room where the scarf hung on the back of the chair.

"Hey," she smiled, pointing at the scarf, "that's right where I left it."

"Okay, how do I look?" Callie smoothed down her white pencil dress that she'd topped with a baby blue cardigan. Her hair was straight with the top pulled back into a knot. "Do you think this is acceptable for a first grader's Star Day? I mean, we'll meet her teachers and all of her friends." She looked up at Jade with pleading eyes.

With her scarf in one hand and a black flat in the other, Jade looked down at her skinny white jeans and black and white striped summer sweater. She looked back at her sister, equally panicked. "How the hell should I know?"

"Jesus, Jade, you're the fashion photographer. What

good are you?" Callie grabbed her clutch and headed toward the door.

"I don't exactly shoot the kid's spring catalog for JC Penney, ya know." She called out to her sister as she slid her other shoe on and followed her outside.

The O'Brien family was coming down the steps of the main house and Callie let out a breath of relief when she saw Lauren also wearing a summer dress.

"Well, don't you two look beautiful!" Eve said as everyone met in the middle of the driveway.

"I'm not sure how we pulled it off, Andy, but we are escorting the four prettiest women in the county to Jefferson Elementary this morning." Trey sauntered up to Callie, wrapping her in his arms and kissing her forehead. "Good morning, sweetheart. How'd you sleep?"

"Not well," Callie admitted.

"Me either. Seems I'm getting kind of used to you in my bed."

"Alright, that's enough. Is nothing sacred with you two? Do you not see your mother standing right here?" Jade shook her head.

"It's okay, honey. When an O'Brien man falls, he falls hard. They are passionate men and it's not in his nature to keep something like that to himself. His daddy was the same way."

"Well, dear God. You'd better put a cap on that before you meet our parents." It was out of Jade's mouth before she could take it back and everyone froze. Everyone but Trey, whose face lit up. "Thanks for the advice, Jade. I'll remember that when your sister takes me to meet your folks."

Andy looked at his watch. "I don't know about you guys, but I don't want the wrath of Miss Alex if we are even one minute late for this thing, so we should probably get going."

"Let me go get the flowers I bought for her and I'll be ready to go." Jade turned, rushing back toward the guesthouse.

Callie looked up at Trey, "Did you remember –"

"Oh shit, baby. I forgot it on the table." He started toward his truck as Callie looked at Lauren and explained, "We bought her a stuffed firefly."

"You're so sweet," Lauren said as Jade rejoined them, "both of you."

Jade laughed, "She's the sweet one," pointing at Callie. "I'm just the sister."

"Well, it seemed Jesse was pretty smitten with just the sister," Andy teased.

"Oh my goodness. You and Jesse? I love that boy." Eve said, clapping her hands excitedly. "And he needs a strong woman exactly like you to keep him in line."

"Whoa, slow down. I only kissed him. It's not like we're engaged or anything. I mean, it was a really, really good kiss, but..." she shook her hands in front of her face, trying to erase the memory that was flooding into her mind. Everyone stood smiling at her, "No. I mean, don't get me wrong, you guys are great, but all of this..." she made a circle above her head with one finger, "no...it's not for me. I'm a city girl, who just so happened to kiss a country boy in the backroom of a restaurant slash bar. A really dreamy country boy who kisses really, really good..."

"Uh huh," Eve and Lauren said teasingly at the same time.

"No. Stop giving me those lovey-dovey eyes." Jade walked to Andy's truck and pulled open the back door. "I am not going there," she announced as she climbed in and slammed the door.

Andy looked at the other two women, "Guess I'm driving," he said with a laugh.

Lauren threaded her arm through his, "I guess so."

Trey pulled up and rolled his window down. "Babe go ahead and ride with them. I'll meet you there."

"Are you sure? I could just ride with you."

"No, I don't want you to be late. Go ahead, I'll be right behind you."

TREY CURSED himself as he drove down the gravel road after picking up the stuffed animal at his house. How could he have forgotten Firefly's present? He smiled remembering how much fun he and Callie had picking it out. Being with her was comfortable and even though he knew there were a lot of things about Callie he didn't know yet, he hoped they would have the rest of their lives to find out everything about each other.

His phone lit up and his throat was suddenly dry. "Hey, Sheriff. How are you?"

"I'm good. How are you, Trey?"

"Not too bad, just heading to the school for Alex's Star Day."

"Oh yeah, my grandson, Trace had his just a few weeks ago and it was about the cutest thing in the world."

"I'm sure it was. What can I do for you today?"

"I've found out some more information on your mama's friend and I think it would be a good idea if I came out to the house and talked it over with you and your family."

Trey's heart pounded wildly in his chest. "Um...you know what Sheriff? I don't think that'll be necessary."

"Now Trey, please listen to me. This is some pretty important information and I'm not sure if Eve is aware of it. It seems suspicious and it's something that could possibly make Callie a threat."

"Sheriff, Callie and I are together."

There was a heavy silence on the other end of the phone, "You mean, you two are dating?"

"Yes, we're dating and I'm hoping it'll turn into something more than that. Something permanent. I'm definitely grateful for everything you've done for me and all the hard work you've –"

"Trey," the sheriff interrupted, "you've got to listen to me."

"There's nothing in Callie's past that will change the way I feel about her. Whatever it is, in time, will come out and we'll deal with it then, as a family."

Trey pulled up in front of the school, shut his truck off, and grabbed the stuffed firefly. "I don't mean to be short, Sheriff, but there are a whole bunch of people I love waiting for me inside of the elementary school and I don't want to be late."

"Trey, I'm sorry but you've left me no choice but to tell you right now over the phone. You need to hear this."

———

TREY WAS SPINNING while the sheriff's words echoed through his head. Everything around him faded as he struggled with each breath. He gripped the steering wheel tightly with one hand as he stared at the phone in his other.

He could still hear the sheriff calling out his name as he

dropped the phone onto the seat next to him. As he walked into the school, he felt nothing – no fear, no anger, just dead space inside. A robot, moving one foot in front of the other, closing in on his family's truth and Callie's lies.

The sound of his boots echoed through the empty hallway as he neared Alex's classroom. He could hear the buzzing chatter of the kids inside and it was then he felt the trembling in his hands. He stepped inside the room and his entire body burned. The sight of his family seated in small chairs in the front of the room was almost more than he could take. A slight sheen of sweat covered his forehead.

Callie looked over her shoulder and greeted him with her stunning smile and all at once, it broke through – her lies, her betrayal. She pointed to the seat she had saved next to her, but he didn't move. His eyes met hers and he hoped his intense stare conveyed the hurt and betrayal he felt. He remained where he stood, her eyes widened and panic flashed across her face. She slowly turned away and he watched as Jade leaned over to her and then glanced back at him with worried eyes.

"Mr. O'Brien. Would you like to take a seat?" the teacher asked. He could only shake his head. The teacher's eyes lingered on him for a few seconds before she nervously cleared her throat and clapped her hands in front of her. "Okay, girls, would you like to go get our Star?"

Three of the girls who were sitting on the floor in the front of the room jumped up giggling and ran from the room. A few seconds later, they escorted Alex back in. She was draped in a red cape with a star crown on her head. She took her place at the front of the room.

"Alex, would you like to introduce your family to your friends?"

Alex nodded as she made a dramatic sweep with her

arm, stopping as she got to Eve. "This is the best grandma in the whole entire world. She bought me a pony and makes me grilled cheese sandwiches whenever I want them. My beautiful mama, Lauren. She's my very best friend and likes to take me camping in our front yard so we can lay under the stars and talk to Daddy. And this is our favorite guy, Andy. He has my back for sure and is always on my side." Alex threw her arms around Andy's neck and made a growling sound like she was hugging him as hard as she could.

Then she side-stepped to stand in front of Callie. "This is my aunt, Callie. Well, she isn't really my aunt yet, but I'm hoping one day my uncle will figure out she's the best thing that'll ever happen to him and give her a big, fat diamond ring, bigger than the moon! And this is Jade, Callie's super cool sister who lives in New York City and buys strings of pearls from the Mob. And, as rumor would have it, kissed Jesse Casey in the backroom of Tipsy's last night."

Jade made a sound like someone had just punched her in the stomach as Alex looked at her, winked, and gave her a thumbs up. The kids sitting on the carpet around them giggled as Jade slumped down in her seat, covering her face.

Alex's teacher rushed to the front of the room, "'Okay, Alex, moving on. What about the gentleman at the back of the room?"

"That's my uncle, Trey. The best uncle in the whole world. He tells me all the time that he loves me most of all. Isn't that right?"

"That's right, Firefly." He walked to the front of the room and bent down on one knee as he handed her the stuffed animal, then leaned in to kiss her cheek. "Don't you ever forget that either."

"Thank you, I love it!" she said as she hugged her new toy.

As Trey stood, Alex turned and pointed to a picture of Jamie on the whiteboard. "And this is my daddy. Wasn't he handsome? He's up in Heaven with the angels but he checks in on my family and me all the time and makes sure nothing happens to any of us."

"How do you know that?" asked a little boy from the front row.

"Well," Alex started in a careful voice, "sometimes when I wake up scared in the middle of the night, I cry for him." She placed a little hand over her heart and continued, "He gives me this warm feeling right here and then puts happy memories in my head. It always makes me feel better. And he does things like sending Andy to me and Mommy. He knew we were going to need someone to take care of us because we are a handful. And just when we thought we were going to lose Uncle Trey, he sent Callie. She loves him so much – it brought him back and now we are all together again."

That's all he could take. Trey turned and stormed out of the room, his heart breaking when he heard Alex yell out his name.

It wasn't but a few steps before he heard her behind him, trying to whisper his name so she wouldn't disturb the other classrooms.

"Trey, wait. Please!"

But he didn't wait, because he didn't want to see her. He didn't want to be anywhere near her right now. Or any of them. He picked up his pace, he needed to get away from her.

"Trey... Can we talk?"

Trey made it to his truck, leaning onto it with both

hands. He dropped his head between his shoulders, trying to slow his breathing and make sense of everything. It just couldn't be. How could this happen?

"Trey, I'm sorry," Callie cried.

He gripped his truck as tight as he could, "Yeah? You're sorry, Cal?" He pressed his forehead against the cold metal of the truck. His stomach twisted into knots. "What are you sorry for? Huh?"

When she didn't respond, he pushed himself off the truck, turning to face her. Callie stood with the help of Jade, who was now trying to comfort her. Eve was there with an arm stretched toward him, her eyes pleading and full of sadness, while Lauren and Andy were rushing out of the school toward them.

"Trey, please. Let's talk about this," Eve begged.

"No, Mom. I'm not talking to anyone but Callie right now, and I asked her a damn question."

He looked back at Callie, "I'm only going to ask one more time. Callie...what are you sorry for?"

He stepped closer to her, his piercing stare never leaving her face. "Are you sorry my brother is dead? Huh? Sorry that he was ripped from his family? From his daughter? Are you sorry about that? Or are you sorry that with everything we've been through in the past few weeks, you forgot to tell me the only reason you're alive is because his heart beats in your chest?"

Callie sagged against her sister. "Yes, everything. I'm sorry for all of it."

"Are you now? Because the way I see it, you're alive because he's dead." His voice cracked, and he covered his mouth as he looked above her head. With a shaky breath and tear-filled eyes, he looked at her and said, "You were supposed to be my future, the person who was going to help me get past this, but instead I'll never be able to look at you the same."

He took a deep breath, letting his shoulders fall. A lone tear slid down his cheek. He raised his arm to the side, shaking his head as he walked backward toward his truck. "Now you're just a walking reminder of everything I'm trying to forget."

Callie rushed to him, "Give me a chance to explain."

"I don't know what's worse, the fact that you lied to me this entire time and obviously got some sort of sick enjoyment out of it, or that you let it go so far that you allowed me to fall in love with you!"

Eve took a step toward her son. "Trey listen to me, this isn't her fault. It's what Callie does. She finds families who have lost loved ones and helps them grieve through the transplant part. I struggled so hard knowing Jamie had given his heart to someone. It didn't seem fair to me. Callie reached out to me on Building Bridges, she didn't know who I was at first, only that I had lost a son. Our stories were so similar, she was hoping she could bring me some peace. It was months before we actually took steps to find out she had been the one to receive your brother's heart."

Trey began pacing, running his hands through his hair and pulling at it, looking to the sky.

"I asked her to come here and help us. To reach out to you and help you see that everything is going to be okay."

"Okay? Are you serious, Ma?" He pointed over the top of his mom, "So that's what this is? You swoop in, make people fall in love with you, and then what? Just up and leave town? Gypsy spirit and all that, right? No roots, no way to track you? You steal my brother's heart and then leave a trail of broken ones in your path?"

"No," Callie choked out a sob, "that's not it at all. I've only ever loved one man."

Trey covered his ears, not wanting to hear her voice anymore. All the emotions were strangling him, the pain in his chest stole his breath and refused to let up. He closed his eyes tightly, shaking his head and letting his anger take over.

"No, listen to me! All of you, right now. From this point on, I died in that alley next to Jamie, like I should have. I don't want to hear from any of you. I don't want to see any of you...ever again. You have all lied and betrayed me! How can I forgive you for that?"

"No, wait, please! I can't let you go." Callie rushed to him, grabbing ahold of his hand. Trey stilled, his jaw grinding as he looked down at their joined hands.

"I don't belong to you anymore," he snarled as he yanked his hand away. "Time to move on, Crazy Girl," he added angrily as he rounded his truck. "You've done enough damage here."

TWENTY-FIVE

It had been forty-eight, horrible hours since Trey had learned the truth about Callie.

She had Jamie's heart. His death had saved her life.

He'd spent the last forty-eight hours fighting against the stabbing pain in his chest. As much as he tried, he couldn't make himself feel any better about it. It was the betrayal and the secrets that hurt him the most. At least that's what he kept telling himself. The aching of raw emotions that swirled around inside of his head was driving him to the edge of sanity.

He jumped from his truck before he barely got the damned thing to a stop. Leaving the truck running and the door wide open, his voice boomed, "Callie! Get out here, damn it! I have something to say to you!" his voice cracking in the middle of her name.

Lauren was the first one out onto the porch and her eyes widened at the sight of him. "No, not you," Trey snapped as he pointed at her. "I haven't even begun to process all the awful things you're responsible for in this shit show I now call my life."

"Callie!" he bellowed once again and then returned his attention to Jamie's widow. "But I guess I deserve everything I got, right, Sis? I mean, it is my fault that Jamie is gone. It's my fault he was taken from you and Alex. Do you feel better now? Vindicated somehow? Now that you've finally hurt me almost as badly as I hurt you?"

Trey waved his hands in front of his face, trying to wipe the vision of Callie's face from his mind like he'd tried doing for the past two days. He needed to get this over with.

"You know what? Never mind. I can't even be mad at you. You're right. I deserved every single bit of this pain I'm going through right now." He pounded a closed fist against his chest a few times, trying to think of something other than the crippling pain that seemed to intensify the longer he went without seeing Callie. "So just go back inside and get Callie for me. I'll say my piece and you'll never have to see me again."

"What's going on?" Andy asked gruffly as he walked out onto the porch.

Trey threw his hands into the air, groaning, "Oh great, and now you. Well since you're here, let's talk about what a jackass you are. You just couldn't wait, could you?"

"What in the hell are you talking about now? Look at yourself. You're a mess, and you need to calm down and lower your voice."

"Yeah, well I wonder how great you would look if you found out the only girl you've ever been in love with didn't actually show up to save you from the hell you've been buried in. But to tell you the reason she's alive is because she took the heart right out of your dead brother's chest!" Trey held his hands up in front of him, "Oh wait, there's more. Your entire family knew, but they just went ahead and let you fall in love with who you thought she was. They let you feel a connection, to become protective of her, and let your guard down...and it never crossed anyone's mind to tell you the truth! How do you think you would feel?"

"You are so self-absorbed!" Andy hollered. "Callie is the girl you fell in love with. She's smart, kind, and a perfect fit in this family...and for some unknown reason, she fell in love with your stupid ass. She is heartbroken because you can't see past this guilt you've surrounded yourself in. Yes, we all knew that Lauren had made the decision to allow Jamie's organs to be donated and it was the hardest thing she's ever done, but after seeing and meeting Callie, why can't you see it wasn't Jamie's death that saved Callie's life, it was Lauren's strength to make that decision. Don't you think your brother would've wanted that?"

"Don't you talk about my brother. I bet the dirt wasn't even settled on his grave before you came sniffing around Lauren. Both of you should be ashamed of yourselves."

LAUREN CRINGED like someone had physically hit her, and Trey watched as her reaction fed Andy's fury. "That's enough," Andy growled while taking a step in front of Lauren. "You want to be an asshole? Fine, be an asshole. But only to me." He glanced over his shoulder at the house. "You leave Lauren and the rest of this family alone and lower your damn voice."

Trey released a forced, cold laugh. "Or what? You're going to kick my ass? Come on down here then."

"Someone should've done this a long time ago," he fumed as he attempted to leave the porch, but Lauren grabbed his arm, pleading with him to stop.

"This is such a waste of time. All I want is Callie!" he raged. He looked past the two standing on the porch and yelled once again. "Are you too afraid to face what you've done to me?"

Eve walked out of the house as calm as could be. "She isn't here, Son," she informed Trey as she wrung her hands in front of her.

A look of anguish crossed Trey's face at the sight of his mom and he wiped his hand over his mouth. He cleared his throat and his voice quieted, but the edge to his tone remained. "What do you mean she isn't here? Where in the hell did she go? When will she be back?"

Eve lifted her chin slightly, keeping her eyes locked on her son. "She's not coming back. She left this morning with Jade. Heading home, I guess, back to the coast."

Trey began to pace, shaking his head and running his hand through his hair. "You're a liar," he accused, pointing a finger in his mother's direction. "She wouldn't leave you guys. Callie! Come out here right now!"

"I'm not lying, Trey."

Trey stopped, his eyes dropped to the ground and he clenched his jaw tightly.

"Son, that girl is in love with you. She may have come for me, but she stayed for you. And now," Eve lifted and dropped her shoulders when Trey's eyes met hers once again, "she's broken and lost. She thinks if she stayed, it would only cause you more pain."

Eve took a deep breath, filling her lungs slowly. "Now you can stand out here and yell her name all day if you want, but it won't do any good. She's gone, and she isn't coming back."

A heavy silence hung between all of them before Trey found the strength to speak again.

"I can't believe you would betray me like this." He shook his head before waving a hand in the air at all of them. "I'm done. I'm done with all of you!" he roared as he turned his back on everything he's ever known and loved. His life, his family...Callie. His stomach twisted into a tight ball as he headed toward his truck with nothing but his mother's sobs floating in the air.

Until the slam of the screen door pinned him to his spot.

Alex O'Brien had heard enough, and she couldn't take one more second of it. She clenched her little fists at her sides and leaned forward, screaming out a sound that stopped Trey in his tracks. He turned quickly, watching as Alex took in another deep breath and screamed at the top of her lungs again.

It was a horrible mix of cries and shrieks and it spoke of everything that had been lost to this precious little girl. She was desperate for a release.

Lauren reached for her, but Andy held her back, and they watched as the littlest O'Brien silenced them all. She stopped for just a second, her shoulders heaving up and down as she gasped for breath, but she was nowhere near done. Her face was red, and tears streamed down her cheeks.

"Why are you all such stupid heads?" she wailed, looking at each of them.

Everyone froze under her gaze. "Why is he leaving us again?" she pointed directly at Trey. "And why can't we all just be a family?"

No one spoke, it had all seemed so clear just a moment ago when Trey was ready to walk away from everyone. But right now, facing down his beloved niece, things seemed clouded and blurred.

"I want an answer and I want one right now," Alex demanded, pointing her finger at the ground and stomping her foot.

"Alex, honey," Lauren whispered.

"No, Mama. No!" She cried loudly. "All of you are messing this up so bad!"

Andy walked up behind Alex and bent down. She spun around, wrapping her arms around his neck as she wept into his chest. He whispered softly to her and gently rubbed her back. He reached a hand out toward Lauren and she gripped it tightly, connecting the three of them.

Trey tried to swallow past the thickness in his throat. He knew Callie had been right about one thing. If it couldn't be Jamie, Andy being Alex's daddy was the next best thing. It didn't mean anyone loved Jamie any less, just that they could love Andy as much and in different ways, for different reasons. And that was all right.

Andy stood as Alex turned back toward everyone and slipped her hand into his. She wanted to be strong but still needed him for support. The three of them stood hand in hand on the porch and Trey's heart stopped as he held his breath. This...this would make his brother happy.

"Go ahead, baby girl. Speak your mind. You have everyone's attention." Andy threw a warning look at Trey, letting him know if he screwed this up, there would be hell to pay.

The little girl took ragged breaths as she tried to speak. "I'm sorry I called you all stupid heads."

She looked up at Andy and he gave her a reassuring smile and a wink.

"I don't know why God and the angels took my daddy."

Lauren covered her mouth, trying to hold in her sobs as tears spilled from her eyes.

"I've spent a lot of nights in my bed praying and trying to figure out why he would leave me. I thought maybe I was too naughty, too sassy, or maybe I didn't tell him I loved him enough."

Alex held her breath, trying to stop crying as she squeezed her eyes shut tightly. "But Andy says that if Daddy would've had a choice, he never would've left me."

Eve nodded, "That's very true. If he could be here with you, he would be." Alex gave her grandmother a smile and a nod before turning back to Trey. "But Uncle Trey, you're going to leave us because you want to. You're choosing it. And you let Callie leave."

"Hold on, Firefly –"

"Shut your mouth, Trey, and let the girl talk," Andy warned between gritted teeth.

Trey shifted his weight from one foot to the other before looking back at his niece and nodding his head.

"You love me, right?" Alex asked.

"Yes, of course, with all my heart," Trey affirmed without hesitation.

"And you love all of us?" she questioned.

Trey swallowed hard. "Yes."

"And you love Callie?"

Trey's voice came soft and broken as he answered her. "Yes, Firefly. I love Callie."

"Then stop messing this up! I know you're mad because we didn't tell you Callie had Daddy's heart, but you don't leave people because you're mad."

"I don't think you understand," Trey said.

"I understand my daddy didn't have a choice or he would've chosen everyone he loves. Because that's what the O'Brien's do. We choose each other over everything else, every time. Grandma tells me that all the time. Is she wrong?"

"No. No, Firefly, that's right," Trey agreed softly as he watched his niece. "That's what we do."

"Good," Alex said as she crossed her arms over her chest

and nodded her head like a decision had been made. "Now stop fighting, stop yelling, stop being a stupid butt, and choose us! Choose Callie and stop leaving all the time. It's really annoying."

Trey let out an unexpected laugh, "Annoying huh?" Trey felt the vice grip on his chest loosen.

"Yes," Alex said, a smile spreading across her tear-stained face.

"I would have to agree," Lauren added, wiping tears from her cheeks and smiling at Trey.

"No one asked you, Sis," Trey said as he pointed at Lauren, a small smile lifting the corners of his mouth. "How about you, Mom? You think I'm annoying?"

Eve shook her head as she walked down the steps toward her youngest son. She leaned back and looked him in the eyes, "No, not annoying. I think stupid butt was a better fit."

Trey leaned down into his mother's comforting hold and for the first time since Jamie's death, he said goodbye to his brother. He said it with apologies to his family, he said it with the tears he finally let run free, and he said it with a promise that he'd never leave them again.

TWENTY-SIX

Callie stood ankle deep in the warm waters of the Atlantic. She wrapped her light-weight cardigan tightly around herself, trying to ward off the light wind that blew around her while digging her toes into the scattering sands below her feet. The world swirled around her in a beautiful mixture of blues and greens and she let herself get lost in it.

Her life had changed so much in such a short amount of time. Even after everything she had been through, Trey O'Brien had been her greatest adventure. But her heart was trapped somewhere between the brilliant sunrise of having been loved by someone like him and the enormous void his absence left.

A storm was coming but she couldn't make herself return to the beach house. She needed the comfort the ocean provided. The promise that even in the worst of times, she had prevailed. She had overcome what would bring most people to their knees, and yet she survived.

In the horizon, where the sky reached down and touched the ocean, she found him. This place where it was almost too far to see, yet somehow went on forever. Where the boundless sky reached down and touched the infinite water. Two things that should never come together, and honestly, never really did, but made something so beautiful and so breathtaking that she was unable to look away.

That was where she would keep her love for him.

She smiled through the pain. Even knowing exactly how it all ended, she wouldn't change a thing. Having Trey for even just a short time, was better than never having experienced him at all.

Her only regret was the pain she had caused him. She wiped away a rogue tear. Taking a deep breath, she hugged herself a little tighter. She was surprised she had any tears left. There had to be a point that physically someone couldn't cry anymore.

"Don't cry, Crazy Girl," said the familiar, husky voice from behind her.

She froze, her stomach twisting and threatening to steal all the breath from her lungs. Slowly, she turned to face the man who would always own her heart.

"What are you doing here?" she asked breathlessly. Her eyes moved over every inch of his face in case this was the last time they would be this close.

Trey's eyes never left hers as he spoke. "This view is pretty breathtaking," he said as he lifted his chin toward her. She glanced over her shoulder for only a moment before turning back to him.

"Yeah, the ocean is pretty amazing."

"I'm not talking about the ocean, Cal."

"Trey, I –"

"The night my brother died..." Trey interrupted, shoving his hands into his front pockets. He closed his eyes tightly and blew out a quick breath, shaking his head and running a hand down his face. "he and I had a talk."

Callie stilled, not wanting to miss a single second of whatever time she had with him. The warm waters rushed up a little higher against the back of her legs, bringing in a string of colder water.

He opened his eyes and found hers, starting a burn in her chest. "He told me he was worried. Worried that Lauren, Mom...all of them...were worried about me."

Callie felt another tear slip down her cheek. Trey's eyebrows pulled together, the color fading from his face. "I didn't listen to him because I thought I knew better, I thought he was just being Jamie. You see, my brother..." he trailed off staring out at the ocean, and she knew he was seeing his brother. He suddenly whispered while shifting his weight from one foot to the other, "God, he would've loved you."

He shook his head slightly as if shaking away the pain of the memory. "My brother was a stubborn SOB. He liked things to go the way he thought they should go. He did everything with determination. He worked hard for his family, he was good at business, he loved hard. And if he loved you, he was loyal. No questions asked, he was on your side."

"He sounds like a wonderful man," Callie whispered.

"He was the best person I've ever known. But that night, he told me if I didn't slow down, I was going to miss the pause."

"The pause?" Callie asked.

A small laugh slipped past Trey's lips and Callie's heart twisted when she saw him smile. "It's when you stop the craziness of life, look around you, and appreciate what you have. Lauren says that people get so caught up in making a life that they never pause to actually live their life. I think she might be onto something."

He took a step, holding out a hand to her. Her entire body relaxed, and a flash of relief crashed down on her. It was all she could do not to whimper as she reached for his hand. He closed the distance between them, taking her hand in his and pulling her close. He pressed his forehead against hers and sighed.

"That night...the night I saw you in the rain, do you know I almost kept driving?"

Callie shook her head, afraid if she uttered a single word, he would stop, and the sound of his voice was the most beautiful thing in the world to her right now.

"I did," Trey kissed the top of her head lightly, "but then I heard his voice. My brother's voice," he took a deep breath in. "He said one word to me, Callie."

"What did he say?"

"He said...pause. I sat in my truck watching you swirl around as the rain fell on you, and I couldn't imagine anything more beautiful. I was out of my truck and standing behind you before I even realized what I was doing, and the moment I touched your skin, I knew. I knew Jamie was right. I was missing everything."

Callie closed her eyes tightly as her chin dropped. Her shoulders shook with the weight of what he was saying and he pulled her in closer.

"I'm not going to lie to you, Callie," Trey hooked a finger under her chin and lifted her eyes to his. "The night he died, I died with him. There will always be some truth to that. I will never be whole again."

"But you were right. It's okay if I let that night change me. I was never meant to be the same person I was before he died. I just couldn't find a way out of the darkness...until you. You are what brought me back. You showed me how other people were moving on, how other people were living their lives without him. Not because it's what they would've chosen to do, but because it's what he would want them to do. Keep living. Keep loving. Keep moving forward. Stay loyal to each other and keep the family together."

He pulled her even closer, slipping his arms around her waist and nuzzling his face into her hair. "You are my pause. In the darkness of the night, on a back road, in the middle of a rainstorm, I paused. And when I did, my life changed. I could no longer just exist without seeing everything that was passing me by."

"I'm so sorry I didn't tell you right away," she apologized.

"There is no way to tell how I would've reacted if you would've told me that first day that you had Jamie's heart. But after thinking about it, I do understand how you got caught up in everything and there wasn't a good time to tell me, or maybe it just didn't feel right? I don't know. But I think once you loved me, the risk was maybe too great. Maybe it was fear of losing what had just begun, fear of being the reason I finally pushed my family completely out of my life?" He kissed her temple and then cupped her cheeks in his hands, pulling back slightly to look into her eyes.

"The one thing I do know, none of this is your fault. You did nothing wrong. You couldn't help the fact that you were born with a faulty heart. You didn't choose to have Jamie's life taken from him so you could continue yours."

She held onto his wrists, needing something to keep her up as she got dizzy with relief. "The only thing you did was fall in love with an O'Brien boy, and just ask my Mama, that's not your fault either because we're pretty irresistible."

Callie playfully swatted at Trey's chest. "Yeah, you are. I can't even argue with you."

He reached between them, running a finger lightly down Callie's scar, her eyelids fluttering at his touch. "I know you have a wanderer's heart, and I know you'll need more than what I can offer. And I also know that it's selfish for me to ask, but I'm asking it anyway."

He reached into his pocket and pulled out a small, velvety black box and lowered down on one knee.

"Come home with me, please. Make a home with me. Better yet, make me your home."

He opened the box containing an antique, square-cut diamond ring. "My Dad gave me this ring right before he died. It belonged to my grandmother. He promised one day I would meet a girl who would make me think I was losing my mind." Trey smiled brightly, pushing his way even further into Callie's heart. "He said she would be beautiful and crazy, strong and independent. All the things it took to love an O'Brien man."

"What he forgot to tell me about was the peace you would bring into my life. The truth is something about you heals my pain. I feel you, Callie." He placed her hand over his heart. "Right here. I feel you whenever you're near. And when you left, it was unbearable pain. What I'm trying to say is, I'm not strong enough to live my life without you."

Callie was quiet even though her dreams were coming true. She had been right; the universe didn't give second chances at life very often. But had been wrong thinking the gift Jamie O'Brien had given her, his heart, was her second chance. Trey was the adventure and the life she had always been searching for. He was her second chance.

Trey pleaded, "Please, Crazy Girl, let me change your last name. Be mine and I will be yours."

The skies suddenly opened, a downpour of rain falling on them. Callie lifted her hands to the heavens and laughed. "Yes! Yes! A thousand times, yes!" She shouted. Trey stood, slipped the ring on her finger before he picked her up and swung her around.

He twirled them in the rain, a dance for everything they had been through, for the future they would have, and for the family he almost let go but Callie somehow pieced back together.

"I've got you," Trey whispered as he held her tightly against his chest.

She kissed his neck and held onto him tightly as she whispered, "And I've got you."

ALSO BY MICKI FREDRICKS

Chasing Jenna

Reckless Fear (The Black Vipers Series Book 1)

Winds of Darkness

visit www.MickiFredricks.com

A NOTE FROM THE AUTHOR

If they'd known about ADHD when I was little, my Ritalin dosage would've been OFF THE CHARTS!!

It goes without saying; I spent A LOT of time by myself after the teacher moved my desk out into the hallway. ** Silver lining** With all that alone time on my hands, I used my imagination to make the world a more interesting place.

When I was little, people said I had an active imagination. In elementary school, teachers called me a daydreamer. My high school counselor said I needed to learn how to focus and my college professors warned me to buckle down if I wanted to be successful.

Before I knew it, it was time to grow up.

So that's what I did. I grew up, got married and had five kids. I work as a full-time nurse, I'm part of the most amazing book-club, blog about books with my best friends and spend my days defusing the drama that only a household full of teenagers could bring.

Oh, and I write a bit when I can and now people call me talented.

Moral of my life story: Hug your kids and embrace their differences. Love them for who they are. Someday, the traits you think are struggles might be exactly what they need to make their dreams come true.

Micki lives in small-town Iowa with her husband, kids and a fat Cocker Spaniel named Joey.

You can find Micki at www.MickiFredricks.com

ACKNOWLEDGMENTS

Thank you to my Lord and Savior, Jesus Christ. Without his grace, I wouldn't make it through this life.

To my husband, Derek. Without you, none of this would matter. You are my why.

To my kids who inspire me every day to be better, push harder and love more deeply.

Lori Rattay: Thank you for your endless hours of reading and re-reading and for your constant encouragement. I'm grateful you never letting me push delete, even when the impulse hits multiple time a day. You are just the best of the best!

Rachel Smith: Thank you for being a constant source of positivity, even when you faced the hardest time in your life. Your strength of character and commitment to your family and faith inspires me every day.

Jen Naumann: I can't believe it took me this long to find you. You're one of my dearest friends and this book wouldn't have happened without the invite to your cabin and your endless encouragement. Thank you for being you and for being a constant in my life.

Anny Van Bockern: Thank you for always being so willing to help. You're an amazing beta reader and you make me laugh like no one else can. You are part of my girl gang and I love you!

Shelby Johnson: Thank you for taking time out of your busy life to proof-read. Your insight made this story even better! Where ever you are in life when my next books comes out, I will find you and I will make you edit! Lol!

Mom and Dad: Thanks for always loving me, even when I'm not lovable. I know you are my biggest fans.

I have the most incredible sister, bothers and sibling in-laws that a girl could be blessed with. Thank you for your endless sharing, liking, promo and encouragement! I love you all so much.

To all the blogs, fellow authors and people who have shared covers, teasers, and given words of encouragement. You will never know how important this is to me. Thank you for being my small village.

Made in the USA
Monee, IL
15 September 2022